Adventures in the Wild Places

J. ALAIN SMITH

Table of Contents

Introduction

THIS IS THE THIRD hunting book I have been able to compose after delving into the darkest recesses of my mind, recalling the latest adventures that I hope you, my loyal reader, will enjoy. You will find in this book that multiple tales have been mined from the same safari or shikar—truly great trips to unforgettable corners of the earth typically create one fantastic adventure after another—each and every waking moment. You don't have to wander too far in the swamps of Tanzania to find something to write about, just as when you get to the top of the Himalayas after days of climbing, odds are, there is going to be something worth talking and writing about when you get back to civilization.

My lucky streak has continued since the publication of my first book, *Close Calls and Hunting Adventures,* and its follow-up, *Hunting New Horizons.* I have been blessed with being able to "live the dream" while hunting in various nooks and crannies around the world, and along the way, collect some truly superb species. The truth is though that while, yes, I am a trophy hunter and I always try to find the biggest prize available, it's really all about the adventure and being in the great outdoors, surrounded by nature in all her glory—*that's* what turns my crank.

Anyone who has had to endure travel, airports, government bureaucracies, the hassles of traveling post-9/11 with firearms, and being away from loved ones for extended periods of time, knows that you have to play this game because you unabashedly love it to the core of your soul—otherwise, you would find something else a wee bit more mundane to keep yourself out of trouble.

My parents raised me and my two brothers in the city, and they made sure that we were able to experience many of life's simple pleasures—camping, fishing, participating in the Boy Scouts—being a family in the most traditional sense—and part of the outdoors whenever we could. That was the start of it all for me, which eventually morphed into big game hunting and real adventure—the pursuit of animals that can bite back.

I hope to someday be able to adequately describe the feeling of staring down some beast that can tear you to pieces, crush you, stampede over you, or ram a tusk or horn through the soft flesh of your lily-white belly. In this book, I give you my best shot so far...

One other thing I want to mention before you get yourself in to a good comfy chair and let your imagination soar. I praise or name certain products throughout my books. I am unique in the hunting book author category, I suppose, because I do not get paid by any company, nor do I receive any paid endorsements, any free or discounted hunts, or get free merchandise for naming products. I'm not knocking writers that do, but it may jade their opinions on products a tad by doing so. So when I state that a certain product is the best I've ever had or used, it is my unbiased opinion. No one's paying me to say anything about that product. It's just that the gear has worked well for me.

You may wonder why I don't use a lot of different equipment or rifles or ammo brands, etc. It's purely because when I find something that works well, I use it, and I keep using it. I can't afford to go to the ends of the earth, spend a small fortune, and then find out that some product can't take the heat of the moment, it's just not worth it to me.

That, and I am a creature of habit...
I hope you enjoy these adventures as much as I did.

J. Alain Smith
Written May 2, 2011, from Seat 2C,
35,000 feet over somewhere.

Benin Buffalo

THE SUN'S EARLY-MORNING RAYS were already heating up the mid-March morning air as Yann Le Bouvier and his two trusted black trackers, Aff and Seidou, followed the dusty tracks of the wounded West African buffalo across the burnt Benin savanna. The errant shot by the old French client the night before had missed all the vital organs Yann was sure, the dark red blood spoor telling the three of them that the bullet had struck meaty flesh only. No sign of the frothy pink blood of a devastating lung shot or the congealed mass quantity of a heart/artery shot splattered about the grass had been evident before they had given up the track as dark cancelled following the spoor any further the night before. This was a gargantuan, healthy bull with massive bosses, the kind clients dream of when they book their safaris to Western Africa.

Most of the time the hunter would have been by Yann's side tracking the wounded bull, closing in on the final stalk, but due to the French octogenarian's age and physical condition, he had remained, wisely, in the Land Cruiser with the driver and Yann's wife, Gwen, this morning, listening to the hiss of the portable radio for the good news that the buff had been found dead not far from where they had left the trail the night before.

But it wasn't close today, and after an hour Yann checked in with Gwen on the two-way radio telling her that they were still on the tracks, having seen nothing yet.

A half hour after the call in, Aff's malarial bloodshot eyes spied a pile of semifresh buffalo dung covering the track he was following. He scraped at it with the toe of his tattered boot, testing the dryness. The thin, brown dry crust of the feces parted, showing a wet dark green interior to the pile.

The wise old tracker stuck his finger in the green mush feeling instantly that the temperature of the dung was not as hot as it should be if the droppings had fallen there within the last hour. Experience told him, however, that the wounded buff could just as well be anywhere nearby at this juncture, since he surely would have found a place to lie up and nurse his aching wounds inflicted on him 12 long hours ago.

The bull had leapt into the air, kicking wildly as the shot pierced his thick black hide, so Aff knew for certain the animal had to be feeling sick from the 300 grain Nosler the client had hit him with and would seek out a safe, thick place to spend the night, waiting, watching his track for any pursuers.

Aff whistled softly to Nwanti, the nickname he had given Yann many years before when they had first started hunting together. Aff, a converted, very successful poacher, worked with Yann, showing him all his bush craft secrets as they hunted side by side, guiding foreign clients and keeping poachers out of their hunting concession. After seeing Yann's uncanny tracking ability in the bush grow daily along with a natural instinct to think like an animal, Aff realized only a poacher like himself could hunt like Yann did, giving him the title "Nwanti," which means *great poacher* in Aff's local language. The name had stuck and now all the villagers and camp staff called him by this name. The mere mention of his name now sent shivers up the spine of poachers and trespassing cattle herders who dared bring their beasts onto Yann's concession as he had a ruthless reputation for severely punishing all violators apprehended.

Aff pointed at the buff doo, signaling with his fingers to Nwanti that the sign was a few hours old, then used his fingers to point at his eyes before pointing two of them toward the bush ahead to show, *"Be careful, the bull could be anywhere."* Yann understood, checking his .458 Winchester one more time, making sure he had a shell in the chamber. This time he decided to leave the safety off, something he rarely did until he saw the quarry, but today, somehow, seemed different.

Another agonizingly slow half hour, easing quietly forward, shoulder to shoulder in the now staggering heat soaring to well over 100 Fahrenheit, brought the three of them to a 5-acre island of 6-foot high dry reed grass, interspersed with thickets of tall thorn-bush, the type of hidey-hole that makes perfect cover for anything up to and including elephants, but especially a nice place to lay and

He's got to be somewhere around here

lick your wounds if you happen to be a pissed off buffalo with a weeping wound in your gut.

Yann glassed the thick stand from 30 yards away, looking for some blood, some sign of where the reeds had been pushed aside, broken over as the bull moved into the morass.

Seidou whispered into Yann's ear, "The wind is right, Nwanti. Let me light the fire and the bull will come out on the right side of the grass."

Yann was just thinking the same thing and got Aff's attention 20 yards to his right with a low whistle. Using sign language to communicate to Aff the plan, the wily old tracker nodded in agreement. Starting the fire along the left side of the island thicket, the wind blowing from left to right would drive any animal hunkered down in the honey hole out into the open.

Yann gave a wave of his hand to Seidou to proceed, then turned to follow Aff, who had his head down scouring the red sandy earth in front of him for any new sign. Yann was shocked when he saw the bull seemingly appear out of thin air as he and Aff rounded the edge of the thicket, the massive beast standing head down, tensed up, intently focused directly on Aff a mere 20 yards in front of him. Yann raised the rifle, at the same time whistling to try to get his trackers' attention, but the bull came now, fast, with no hesitation.

Yann's shot was a good one considering the 45-degree angle the bull was giving him as it charged toward the unarmed Aff. As the big .458 boomed and the 500 grain bullet struck the bull's near front shoulder, the animal immediately changed its focus, now coming head-on for Yann as he jacked another bullet into the chamber of the mighty bolt action, raising the open sights level again until they settled squarely on the fast-approaching deadly head.

With the bull keeping its nose low, the thick massive boss of horn covering the brain below, Yann made the split-second decision to go for the spine behind the head where the Brahma-style hump rises slightly on the shoulders. Squeezing the 3-pound pull trigger, the recoil sent the rifle barrel upward 6 inches blocking his view temporarily, while noting with cold fear that the shot had not had the desired crippling effect intended and that the buffalo was still coming. He had missed the spine by a mere fraction of an inch...

As Yann tried frantically to jack another round into the rifle, time began to slow down, as if the world had gone into slow motion and he knew that he would never complete the split-second procedure before the bull crashed into him.

Instinct, remaining cool under pressure, and being in top-notch physical condition, not an ounce of fat on Yann's 5-foot-10-inch frame from years of working in bush, still did not give the soon-to-be pulverized Monsieur Le Bouvier a great deal of choices about his future.

Holding the rifle, its bolt still open, with both hands, Yann smashed the weapon forward onto the bull's 35-inch wide horns just at the same moment as the great bull slammed his horns upward in the classic buffalo-hooking motion. The rifle protected Yann's guts on the first hooking action, but the fiberglass stock slammed into the guide's chest, instantly breaking three ribs on Yann's left side. He was up in the air now as if he'd made a bad jump on a trampoline, spinning out of control, the rifle lost from his grasp, the bull watching and waiting for him as he descended back toward terra firma.

The buff hooked at him with its deadly horns before he hit the ground, the left horn tip catching the inside of Yann's webbed ammo belt, leaving him dangling upside down, all his body weight crushing against the bull's horn. The enraged bull flicked Yann back up into the air with the ease of a child tossing a ragdoll.

Yann tried to grab at tree branches as he crested 12 feet in the air, the spindly thorn branches giving way as he fell awkwardly downward again to the infuriated bull who this time didn't miss and drove his left horn through Yann's ribs, splitting them cleanly as if a razor had been used, before driving the horn deeper with a quick flick of his head into the professional hunter's lung. The wind was knocked out of him, literally, while a hissing sound emerged from the hole in Yann's side as the bull threw him in the air one more time.

Yann was in a state of shock at this point and wondered why nothing hurt. He felt blood on his side as he struggled to catch his breath, arching in a high cartwheel over the bull, but his mind was still very aware of his circumstances. The rifle lay below him.

If I could just get my hands on it when I land, I could put the one remaining bullet in the rifle into the snorting bastard's brain, he thought.

The bull expertly shifted his position to catch the gangly human with a right hook with the blood-covered point of horn as Yann's hips landed on the bull's shoulders. The horn tip drove easily into the unlucky Frenchman's face, splitting the cheek flesh into a V-shaped wound, breaking teeth and heavily bruising the roof of Yann's mouth.

His body lay prone on the bull's back, with his belly up, when the buff angrily twisted his head, the horn tearing loose from the cheek, skidding his nemesis across the ground until Yann was lying on his back, his legs spread-eagled, his feet facing the panting bloody bull, in what can only be described by a man as being the most vulnerable position any guy can be in.

Before Yann could react, the bull surged forward, stepping on his exposed legs as he did, before driving his left horn into Yann's fully exposed crotch, yanking its head up violently, attempting to toss him once more. Yann, in a natural reaction to having one's private parts rearranged, held onto the right horn tip with his right hand while his left held on rodeo-style to the muddy, gnarly bosses.

The dusty black bovine seemed to weaken somewhat at this stage, staggering with the full weight of the man upon his neck. The buffalo bucked his back legs up, jerking his head forward, his horn tearing loose from Nwanti's crotch, sliding the PH across the dirt on his belly, stopping 6 yards in front of the bull.

Yann didn't move; he wasn't sure if he could. He wanted to look up to see where the bull was, where his rifle was—*was it within reach?*—but somehow he knew the best thing was to remain still and play dead. For that matter, Yann wasn't sure at this point if he was still alive or not, a sense of euphoric shock had taken all the pain away. He felt himself floating in a blissful mist.

Is this what they talk about? This is that feeling right before you go to heaven? What a beautiful sensation.

The image of his lovely wife suddenly appeared in his tattered mind, then his daughter, the love of his life. He didn't want to leave them, not yet. There was so much still to do in life, to see his little girl grow up, to make a life together with his family after his professional hunting career was finished, and now that would be soon...

Hot foul breath brought Yann back to reality as the bull pressed its sandpaper-like whiskered muzzle up against the gaping hole in his cheek, blood trickling out of it onto the gray ashen soil. He realized at this point that there was a wad of salty sticky fluid inside his mouth as well.

Playing dead is working well, Yann thought as the bloody, spittle-covered muzzle backed away from his limited field of vision, giving him hope that the mauling was over.

His optimism was put on hold when a gargle of pain hissed out of the torn flesh of Yann's cheek a few seconds later when the bull suddenly decided to give him a few more blows with his horns just for good measure.

Using his massive weight, the buff pushed his hard, solid bosses down on Yann's legs, starting at the calves and working his way up to his back, driving him time after time into the hard earth. Head butting him over and over in the lower back region while intentionally stepping with his sharp hooves onto the hunter's legs, the bull was just being plain old-fashioned mean at this point, seeking and acquiring revenge for the searing pain wracking his own body from the bullets tearing up his insides.

Now, after not reacting to the trashing from the bull's bosses and simply lying still, expecting the next thrust of horn somewhere else in his flesh at any moment to kill him, there was suddenly a stop to the thrashing, a strange quiet engulfing the morning air. The sound of his trackers yelling French curses at the bull got his attention, giving him some semblance of hope. A few moments later, he felt Aff tugging at his good arm whispering, "Patron, the bull is dead. It is dead, Nwanti."

With that, Yann tried to stand up with no luck as Aff assisted with a helping hand and Seidou retrieved the Winchester, hustling it back to rest against the tree that Yann crawled over to, the shade giving him some respite from the now-glaring sun.

Seeing the buff was truly dead and doing a quick inventory of his body, Yann realized that he was in dire straits. Out of his torn shirt hung a chuck of pink lung, his legs had been ripped open in various places, a deep, gaping wound in his crotch made him not want to look at the details, and he could tell by the look on the faces of his trusted trackers that he must look like hell. Everywhere was blood, but it was hard to tell what was buffalo blood and what was French. Dark burgundy smeared and oozed across every inch of his broken body.

Handing the small radio to Aff he told him to contact the madame and have the truck brought quickly to him.

Aff tried the two-way radio, but they were too far away from each other for reception, even when the sharp old tracker climbed up a tall tree to see if that would give him some contact. However, nothing but static responded to his calls.

Desperate and running out of time as the ground around him turned a dark red Yann told Aff, "Go to the madame and bring her here. Do not tell her what happened; only to hurry as fast as the driver can go. Tell her we had some trouble with a buff and to get here now."

"Oui, Patron," Aff yelled as he turned and began running the 45 minutes toward where they had left the truck, taking one last glance at the buffalo, spitting on it as he ran past.

Yann sat in the shade, a sedate calm blanketing him against the pain that would surely come any moment, his mind wandering once again to Gwen and his little girl. It occurred to him that he wasn't afraid of dying; it was inevitable by the looks of things. But he was concerned about his wife and daughter's future without him and how his daughter would have to go through life without the guiding hand and love of a father.

He began to reminisce about the good times, recollecting special moments with Gwen, about his parents and his childhood, when it dawned on him that he was actually seeing his life flash before his very eyes, just like they say in the stories and movies, right before you die.

"Seidou, come here," he hissed through the gaping hole in his cheek. Seidou leaned in close so Bwana Nwanti would not have to exert much effort to speak.

"You tell the madame that I died quickly, you understand? That there was no pain. Tell her that I said I loved her and our daughter more than anything in the whole world, and that I am sorry. Sorry for not being with them in the future, to take care of them, will you?"

The tough young French PH's vision blurred as tears filled his eyes, not with tears of pain, but of pure love, of love soon to be lost forever.

Seidou shook his head. "Nwanti, you will not die; you can not die. We all need you to be strong. You are the patron, and people depend on you. The truck will be here soon. Hold on to me, Nwanti, Do not go. Hold on."

The Frenchman slipped in and out of consciousness, while Seidou, who had also taught him many secrets of Western Africa's bushland, who had shown him the secret waterholes near the park boundaries where solo "dugga boys" would lay up in the midday heat, the same man who had mentored him as if he were his son, continued talking and encouraging him to stay awake, to stay alive, but finally, Yann reached his limit.

Attempting to speak through his blood-filled mouth, air hissing with each breath, escaping out of the chasm in his left cheek and the fist-sized hole in his chest, he whispered, "I think I'm done, my friend. I can't hold on."

"No, Nwanti, listen! I hear the truck! Listen, I can hear Aff yelling directions. They are close! Do you hear him? He is coming; the madame is coming. You must be strong for her, Nwanti," Seidou pleaded as he stood up and yelled while waving his arms at the approaching vehicle.

I think I do hear the truck, don't I? Yes, I hear it now; I'm going to make it. I will make it...I will make it, damn it.

In an attempt at brevity, only thanks to Gwen's impromptu nursing, his dedicated safari team, a couple of excellent local doctors who stabilized him enough to make it to the hospital in town, and more luck than a Leprechaun has on Saint Patrick's Day, Yann Le Bouvier not only survived the buffalo mauling, but after many surgeries and agonizing recovery time in France, he returned to hunt buffalo in Africa, *5 short months later.* Some guys never learn...

Sequel

I weaseled the above story out of Yann after plying him with a few too many Panjori Punches, the magical rum and fresh squeezed pineapple concoction Dennis Anderson and I invented while hunting with Yann in Benin in 2010.

The next morning, you can imagine the trepidation Yann and I felt when we stumbled upon the tracks of another solitary bull. By then, I wished I had not drunk the last couple Panjori Punishers (as they had been renamed at breakfast).

It was day 10 of a 14-day mixed bag hunt for some unique species only found in West Africa. By this time, a Nagor reedbuck, Western hartebeest, Western kob, and Harnessed bushbuck had all fallen to my trusty .7 mm thanks to some better-than-normal shooting on my part.

We had hunted hard for the Western savanna buffalo every day, but had ended empty-handed due to a variety of evils.

One day, really big tracks led to the Panjari Park boundary. Unfortunately, you can't follow them into the park. Another day, two dugga boys we tracked decided to wander over to the concession next door. Twice we followed sets of three bulls' fresh steaming piles of green dung, only to have them join up with herds of females and young. After catching up to them and sorting through the herd, we found only soft bossed bulls, nothing worth shipping back to Seattle to be permanently enshrined on the wall of fame that awaits beasts of their ilk.

This day as we set out from camp at 5:30 A.M. one tracker was looking for tracks crossing the so-called road while perched on the front left fender of the rickety Land Cruiser. Dawn warmed rosily in the east, and a sense of "time is running out on this safari" permeated the back of the truck where I scanned the passing bush for signs of life. This was a new road, not one we had taken before; one with promise, I felt, as we wove through the thorny brush.

Suddenly, Yann tapped on the roof, signaling the driver to a halt, and the tracking crew of three fanned out around the secluded waterhole where we had stopped. A bevy of Guinea fowl scattered at our

*Yann and I taking a break from the heat while our driver is
watering the plants*

approach. Francolins chattered as they scrambled away from their
morning drink. I tightened my leather ammo belt one notch, happily
noting that all the past weeks walking had shed some baby fat, then
checked my bullet count, confirming that I had indeed replenished
my supply after a superb baboon shoot the evening before.

All was in order as the lead tracker, a strong, thickly muscled
African named Laurent, came jogging back to the truck, letting us
know there were fresh tracks of a lone bull on the other side of the
pond. Within seconds, we were on the ground and following him,
raring to go. It was still cool by Western Africa standards, hovering
somewhere near one hundred, but still more civil than the 120 degrees we could look forward to at three each afternoon.

Laurent had certainly found a hot track. The beast had just
peed within the last 10 minutes. The ground was still wet and warm

where he left his mark. Fifty yards further, as we eased along getting acquainted with the spoor, a barely glazed-over pile of dugga dung glowed on the track. Everyone knew he had to be near; knew we were going to get a good look at this one.

The slight breeze wafted toward us from the north, and I could instinctively tell the bull was wandering back to the safety and shade of the park, grazing leisurely as he meandered about.

Yann glanced over at me with a devilish grin on his sunburned face, thumbs-up; showtime. I checked my rifle making sure for the fourth time that I had a bullet in the chamber, clicked the safety back on, easing forward to the left of the trackers so I would have a clear field of fire when we saw the bull. Glancing back at Yann, I wondered what must go through his mind as he closed in on the same species that had so ravaged him not that long ago. Hell, the damn thing would have killed him had it not been for the fact that it just wasn't his time to go. That, plus a good deal of luck, and a woman that wouldn't let him die in her arms.

I've been in on over 20 buffalo kills, mostly of the Cape variety, never having faced what you would really call a full-on charge by one, but I've been through plenty of false charges, stampedes, etc., and watched bulls take a barrage of a couple thousand grains of lead and shake them off as if they were mere BBs.

Suddenly at this point, though, for some strange reason, I was afraid—really afraid. I hate to admit it, but it's true. Perhaps it was hearing firsthand how a buffalo had ripped to shreds the man walking 20 feet away from me. Or perhaps it was the sleepless night I had, wondering why bad things happen to good people, and why I, who may not necessarily fall into that category, had been spared being mauled, gored, or had any spontaneous reconstruction surgery performed in the bush on my physique so far. Was it just that it had not been my time yet? Or my trouble clock ticking closer to some cosmic preset alarm out of my control? Would that alarm go off today? I should have brought my .375 H&H instead of the .7 mm peashooter I carried now, I realized.

Trying to calm my nerves, it dawned on me that I had, in fact, recently killed a Nile buffalo dead on his feet, with two quick shots from the same rifle only months before, so I had not considered it to be an issue on these, the second smallest of the African buffalo species, surpassed in diminutive stature by only the aptly named Dwarf buffalo. After last night's tale of horror, though, my mind would have been saner and my nerves a lot less shaky had I been carrying my trusty old Alex Henry .577 Nitro double rifle.

Aff, tracking to the right, let out a low whistle getting everyone's attention and pointing to a steaming pile of crap, which appeared to have exited the rear end of a buff only minutes before. As he and Laurent stayed on the obvious hot track, I watched in front of us for any sign of the black beast: an ear flicker, a tail twitch, oxpeckers, anything.

The trackers began to swing around as the tracks led in a half circle back toward the waterhole. Yann looked over at me and made the motion that the bull had lain down somewhere directly in front of us and to be ready.

"No problem, Yann." I had never been so ready for anything in my life, for criminy sakes!

As we followed the spoor's circuitous route, the breeze was now passing from our backs into the large island of 5-foot high reed grass covered in shade by a grove of ancient acacia trees that lay 60 yards straight-ahead.

If I were a buffalo, that's exactly where I would lay up for my siesta, I thought, when suddenly, all hell broke loose from the grass thicket. Guinea fowl exploded into the air, cackling and raising hell as the brushy patch erupted and a huge black buffalo bull charged out, running full tilt toward the park and safety.

Yann shouted, "Shoot, shoot," as the buff ran zigzagging through the trees. I found him in my scope, put the crosshairs level with the middle of his mighty frame, and waited for an opening to shoot.

Now! No, a tree's in the way. Nowww. Wait! Tree. Not yet. Another tree. Don't shoot yet. Now. No, wait, I thought, holding the running bull level in my scope as he broadsided us, moving to my right.

"Now," I hissed, squeezing off a shot, holding just below his chin, leading him like you would a mallard passing over decoys as his shoulder passed the last tree. A whoop from the boys told me I hit him, and I distinctly heard the slap of the bullet connecting with flesh, but I was shocked to see the impact the 165 grain Barnes had on the buff. It knocked the bull off his feet, his forward motion launching him into a head-over-heels somersault. The buffalo was down, but still thrashing the ground as Yann and I ran up to him, Yann covering him with his .458 as I finished his thrashing with

Everyone is happy once a bull is down for good

another Barnes Triple-Shock through the spine and boiler room from close range. The mighty beast was dead.

A lot of backslapping and the usual festive exchange that accompanies the culmination of a successful hunt was mixed with excitement at the size of the bull's horns, especially since there hadn't been much time for judging his head gear as he bolted from the thicket.

As we settled in, getting ready to take pictures after the truck showed up with our gear and the cool box, I looked over at Yann, studying him discreetly through the veil of my Aviators, not seeing anything but joy and pride in his demeanor. No fear, no remorse, no need to go over and kick the bull or cut his testicles off as some might feel a need to do after all he'd been through.

Sometimes you get lucky

Affissou, the always cheery driver, handed me a beer in congratulations. It was still early in the day, but we figured we had earned one.

"You are sniper," Affissou laughed in broken English as I toasted him and the boys with the lukewarm beer. The rest of the guys laughed along as he translated what he had said to me. I began to walk toward the shade, turning my back to them as I raised the beer to my lips, hoping none of them would see my hand shaking as I raised the bottle for a most welcome swig.

Yann and I with a Top Ten buff

Kashmir Markhor

WHILE I WAS HUNTING in Pakistan in early 2011, an opportunity presented itself to collect a second specie of the Markhor, the Kashmir variety, located in the northern reaches of the country in the tribal area known as Khoisitan. This fine trophy differs from his cousin further south in that it is a much-larger-bodied animal than the Suleiman and carries a completely different horn structure. The Kashmir Markhor's headgear resembles a kudu-type "flared horn" instead of the tight corkscrew horn of its southern family member.

I was quickly running out of time on this hunt, having been away from home for more than 3 weeks already. I had commitments stateside requiring me to be on a plane, no matter what, at the end of the week.

The problem with the delays on this trip had all revolved around the Karakoram Highway being impassable due to a series of slides, avalanches, and washouts from the recent heavy rains and snows that had plagued the mountains where the road winds through. The "Highway" (calling it that is the equivalent to calling a kite an airplane) follows the course of the Indus River from its source in the Himalayas to its final destination, dumping into the Indian Ocean at the southern coastline of Pakistan at the city of Karachi.

The historical roadway has been referred to as the Silk Road for centuries. It was the major trading thoroughfare linking the spices and trade goods of India and Pakistan with the silk and treasures of China. Originally a simple trail traversed by camel, donkey, and yak, winding through one of the few passable high valleys the Himalayan massif concedes, it now handles thousands of trucks and automobiles daily, *when it is passable.*

Carved into steep cliffs and mountains, cascading down to the mighty Indus, its very structure confirms that it is always going to be a one-lane road each way, wracked on a constant basis by massive rock slides playing havoc on the paved twists and turns where the idea of guard rails to protect vehicles from a half-mile plunge into the frothy river below has not caught on yet.

Ejaz Ali, my guide, interpreter, and all-around good guy, and I began the journey to the Kashmir Markhor's haunts, leaving Islamabad midday, when word finally came to us that the Karakoram Highway had been cleared and was now passable after being shut down for over a week. Knowing from the beginning that we would only have 6 days until we had to be back in Islamabad so I could catch my flight home, we decided to give it a try anyhow. There was definitely not enough time to pursue one of the toughest trophies in the world in some of the worst climatic conditions anywhere, but we gave it a try regardless. Logic had no foothold on the slippery slopes of my overly ambitious persona.

Kaan Karakaya, who booked the hunt through his company Shikar Safaris, had warned me over the phone before I left Islamabad that the last guy who had hunted where I was going had shot an average male on day 14 of a 14-day hunt, the weather and the terrain having made for an excruciating chase.

The driver we hired for the journey to the small town of Dassu had a four-wheel, four-door pickup truck, so we could load our gear, food, and camping equipment comfortably in the back. The long roll of mountaineering rope had me puzzled until Ejaz explained.

"It's pretty steep in places, and sometimes we need to use ropes and pitons to access some of the hunting spots."

Hmmmm. This should be interesting, I thought as I stared out the window, trying to keep myself amused, my imagination and my iPod keeping me company for the long drive that lay before us.

Nine hours and 250 kilometers later, we stopped for the night at a small town named Besham with a decent motel on the banks of the Indus to catch a little shut-eye while avoiding the drive on the Karakoram in the darkness. The road is bad enough in the daylight, but is extremely dangerous at night.

We rose at dawn the next morning and were soon on the road, rolling into the village of Dassu at 8:30 in the morning to find, much to my pleasant surprise, our whole hunting crew of 20 porters, wildlife officials, scouts, the cook and helpers all ready to go,

The Highway

waiting for us. Being used to having to "inspire" the help on Asian hunts to get it into gear, this proved to be a great start. Falqoos, our headman and local tribal leader, told me through Ejaz's translations that we had a 4-hour climb ahead of us and we needed to get going.

"Let's go then!" I replied as I turned to begin the long rocky adventure following a tributary of the Indus that cascades through the valley we were destined to hunt in.

Not an hour's hike from the village I beheld one of the strangest wildlife scenes I have ever witnessed as we came around a fractured cliff. There, on the snowy cliffs of the river, perched on an outcropping jutting over the raging torrent, sat a band of a dozen monkeys! Not exactly what you think of when you are in wild goat country. These hairy, bald-faced simians must have somehow gotten lost on their way to warmer climes I figured, since I didn't see a banana tree anywhere in sight. We filmed them as they went about their monkey business, paying no attention to us, grooming each other in the warmth of the morning rays of the sun peeking over the horizon. Over the next few days we saw several other troops of the big monkeys.

Our gang finally arrived at a small wood and stone cabin with a wood-fired stove in the middle of it. It had been built into the cliffs a thousand yards above the river. I realized that it would be a little cozy since it would be serving as our home for the next few days. Each member of our troop began staking out his territory on the straw-mat-covered floor. I secured a good corner position where Ejaz and I would have a little more elbow room than the rest and put my pack down before leaning the rifle safely in the corner behind me.

A quick hot lunch of domestic goat stew—including most of the internal organs as an added bonus—was whipped up before we

The guides eating in the cabin. Only use your right hand for dipping in the communal bowl...

continued our climb up the mountain to a perfect lookout where we could glass the surrounding mountains.

Fog and clouds rolled in and out of the valley. One minute you could see for miles; the next, you couldn't see the guy next to you. Ejaz translated to me that Falqoos said that they had been watching several big male Markhor in this valley, one with the typical horn formation, another with a very wide V-shaped flare, and another old, heavy-horned veteran that may be 50 inches long.

I looked back at Ejaz and whispered, "Fifty inch horns? Are you kidding?"

"That's what they say. The old guy with the white hair and beard over there that they call Uncle, says he saw him 2 days ago

Markhor terrain

just above us at the tree line. See that big snowfield up against the gray rock face, right there? They say the Markhor males don't move around much this time of year so we may see him again, but all of the ones they have described are shooters."

My excitement was immediately tempered as the hillside once again became totally socked in and stayed that way the rest of the day.

The cabin and Uncle

Day 2 found us back in the same spot with overcast cold skies threatening to soak us at any minute as we all glassed the chasms and cliffs, searching for Markhor. The search was constantly being interrupted by the clouds and fog drifting in and out of the valley. It seemed that all the hillsides would clear up regularly for us to glass, except the one above us that held the big Markhors the crew had seen there previously. It wasn't until late in the afternoon that we finally got an hour straight break in the clouds to do some serious searching.

Suddenly "Uncle," became excited, motioning for us to bring him the spotting scope. Setting it up, he quickly zoomed in on what he had seen. As I got behind the eyepiece gazing through my Swarovski set at 20 power, I beheld a sight reserved for few mortals—the biggest Kashmir Markhor I had ever seen. I mean *bigger*

than any picture of one I had ever seen. As with all really huge trophies, no matter what the species, one look usually tells you right
away that this is a monster, and this old boy was no exception to
that rule.

It was four o'clock already, and after some high-strung jabbering among the troops, it was decided that we could not reach where
he was feeding before dark. I voted for going for him. What the
hell, I only had 1 hunting day left after today, and I wasn't afraid of
the dark, but I was overruled by the more sensible locals who had a
much better idea of what was involved in reaching him from where
we stood. Their decision was buoyed when another wave of cumu-
lous wafted into the valley, obscuring our chances of finding him
again. I was feeling very frustrated, to put it mildly, sitting, doing
nothing, knowing the big one was a couple hours away from us and
there was not a damn thing I could do about it.

The clouds began to thin out a half hour later, when suddenly
Falqoos grabbed the spotting scope and set it up facing directly
above us. Getting a good look at what he had seen through the
scope, I found another big Markhor feeding down the mountain
toward us. He was not as big as the monster that had been to our
left, but I hesitantly began weighing my options as I realized this
one may come into range.

*Al, you have 1 more day after this to hunt. The weather has been
and will probably continue to be lousy. This Markhor is no slouch,
probably in the 45- to 46-inch range and old, but certainly not in the
same league as the other one. You should do the wise thing and go after
the bird in the hand and ignore the ones in the bush. The big one could
be long gone by tomorrow.*

I looked over at Falqoos who had every intention of getting me
to shoot the one above us. The hell with the other one. I reluctantly
agreed to take him if he came further downhill. I suggested that
we climb higher to close the gap, seeing that there was a very good

approach to him if we climbed around a sheer cliff face to our right. This would get us to within 1,000 yards, and if the billy continued to come downhill, he would eventually be within whacking range.

Falqoos and the others didn't like the idea of moving, telling me to relax and wait, the Markhor would come to us. Ejaz translated that the locals knew this one's habits, and they were sure he would end up on the small patch of steep grassy pasture clinging to the barren rock wall 350 yards above us. I looked at my watch. Mickey's hands pointed at 5. Knowing it would be dark at 6:30, I didn't like the odds of this scenario occurring and told everyone so.

"Let's go up there right now and get closer. He won't see us, and the wind is perfect," I pleaded.

"Relax, be patient," I was told by the Khosimen tribal elders, sitting out of the wind with their customary wool hats and scarves, looking like so many Afghan rebels from a *National Geographic* magazine.

Long story short, half an hour later, the Markhor decided to take a right turn, wandering toward where the big guy had been seen. At that point, I would have given anything to be fluent in their language so I could have stood on the side of the mountain and yelled at the top of my lungs to the assembled tribe, "I TOLD YOU SO!"

No one said a word; no one needed to, as we slid and slipped our way down the scary excuse for a trail in the pitch-black darkness, arriving back at the crowded cabin an hour and a half later.

Around the woodstove that night, Ejaz and the locals came up with a last-day plan, relayed to me as I sulked in the corner, nursing my aching legs, my knees reminding me of every cheap shot I'd ever been the recipient of in my old soccer playing days, pissed at the world over not having shot the Markhor.

"We will get up at 3:30 and climb toward where we saw the big one, assuming the weather will permit us. The guys say that we will be in a good spot when dawn arrives to see if he has stayed where we last saw him. By going early, we should be able to hunt quite a bit before the fog rolls in. You OK with that plan?" Ejaz quietly asked, the rest of the room staring at me, silently waiting for an answer.

"Sounds great. I like the idea. We might as well get in as much hunting time as is possible since tomorrow is it, right?"

My reply was translated to the assembled tribesmen. A collective sigh of relief escaped before they each took turns doing their evening prayers, facing Mecca on the small rugs in the corner of the cabin. When prayers were finished, each guy began to find some floor to curl up on since our departure was only going to give us 5 short hours of sleep.

Three small cups of the local tea and spiced milk, a handful of dry, sweet biscuits, and I was waiting outside in clear, star-filled skies for the rest of the crew to get their proverbial act together at 4 A.M. It was a good sign that the lousy weather we had been putting up with for the last 3 weeks was finally taking a turn for the better. The waxing moon had come over the horizon, shedding light strong enough to read a novel by and giving us plenty enough for climbing. The last thing we needed was a gaggle of flashlights bobbing up the mountainside toward our target, although I think Ejaz and I were the only ones who had a flashlight...

Sitting on a log under a snarly oak tree 2 hours later, surrounded by brush and moss-covered boulders, I was shivering from the cold that arrives just before dawn. I wore every piece of clothing I had with me, as well as my rain gear on, but could still feel the bitter bite nipping at my bones.

Falqoos, feeling much the same by the way he was stomping around after glassing the opposing hillside, made hand signals indicating we should climb some more. Our entourage complied immediately—anything besides sitting here freezing!

Twenty warming minutes later, Falqoos called a halt to our ascent when we came to a jumble of giant boulders covered in a crusty snow, the sun now peeking over the ridge warming our backs. He and Uncle began glassing the canyon that was now visible from our new lookout point.

Since the guides were insistent on using my binos, since they had none, I sat behind them, glancing over their shoulders and thanking God for sunny skies and a beautiful morning. I was day-dreaming about whether we would still be able to find the one we had not shot yesterday afternoon, in case we couldn't find Mr. Big, when Falqoos excitedly turned to Ejaz and me and asked for the spotting scope. Uncle saw something as well and handed me back my binoculars, pointing to a rocky cliff face, with one ancient pine tree jutting out of the scree, hanging on to life by a pair of ancient roots.

It took me a minute to find what had them so jacked up. One of the drawbacks of communication breakdowns when you have multiple languages all competing with one another is the panic that ensues when Mr. Big shows himself. But there he was, standing to the right of the tree, only his head and shoulders exposed, enjoying the sun as much as any of us. There was no mistaking it was him, his long, massive, curling horns pointing skyward as he regally surveyed his empire.

I used the range finder on my Leica 10 x 42's to get a reading of 401 yards, a long ways away, maybe too long. The crew were all trying to get a look at the magnificent creature, causing way too much commotion, until Ejaz gave them all a *"shush, relax."* It had the desired effect of shutting them all up and bringing a temporary calm to the AK 47-packing lads.

Falqoos motioned for me to hurry up and shoot, but I tried to remain calm and scratched the distance into the snow on the boulder we were lying on, implying it was too far. He shrugged his shoulders and smiled a wry little grin as if to say, *"There he is, Pasha Smith. You wanted him, you got him, and, oh, by the way, it's the last day, you chicken."*

I grabbed my rifle, quietly slipping around into the throat of the barrel, then easing it up over the crest of the rocks and finding a superb rest in the snow. Ejaz handed me my daypack to support my right elbow as I settled in behind my Bansner .7 mm, finding the Markhor standing in the rock-solid crosshairs.

The goat made my decision much easier for me when he thankfully decided to stroll out onto the rocky sunlit ledge, coming to halt, standing perfectly broadside.

I did my best to control my rattled nerves, but I have to admit I had buck fever bad as I anchored the 400-yard crosshair behind his shoulder. The rest I had in the snow was so perfect all I had to do was squeeze the trigger. I told anyone who was listening, "Get ready, I'm going to shoot."

"The camera is rolling," came the reply from Ejaz.

If you've killed much stuff with a rifle, you know when the shot feels good, and this was one of those good times. The Markhor staggered before jumping onto a ledge with the old pine tree silhouetted behind him. I jacked another round in, but hurried the shot, striking the tree just over the line of his back. Luckily, the impact of the bullet scared the bejesus out of him, and he leapt back onto the rocky cliff face once again.

I could see through the scope as I settled in for shot number three that he was seriously hurt and was just about to shoot him again when excited chatter erupted all around me and the distinctive sound of an AK 47 having a round jacked into it interrupted my plan. Uncle had his AK pointed over the rocks at the Markhor, while Ejaz railed on him to put it down. Seems old Uncle figured he'd get in on the action, even if he only had open sights and the animal was 400 yards away.

I hissed at him, "No, no. No shoot," while I shook my fist at him. He understood, but the dejected look on his face was somewhat humorous as I tried to find the Markhor in my scope once again. I finally found him still standing, his head swaying from one side to the other, hurt bad. Me, being a proponent of the school of thought that you should keep throwing lead in the air until the beast is down for good, sent one more merciful 160 grain Barnes Triple-Shock at him, crushing him on impact and sending him tumbling down the hill to the jubilant delight of everyone on the mountainside.

Uncle and one of his sons took off immediately to find him, while we gathered up our stuff before beginning to pick our way slowly across the sheer mountainside, slipping in the snow, whacking my knee on a sharp chunk of shale, Ejaz twisting his ankle, all

Kudu-style horns on a goat

of us holding on for dear life, but otherwise enjoying every thrilling moment as we worked our treacherous way down to our prize.

Thirty minutes later after some of the hairiest rock climbing I've ever done, I finally got to put my hands on what may be the new world record Kashmir Markhor.

Is this steep enough?

All the guides with the goat

Swimming in the Swamp

S PIRAL-HORNED ANTELOPE HOLD A special place in most big game hunters' hearts. There is something about the elegant twist of their headgear; the ivory tips topping off the daggerlike shafts and the way the antelope carry them regally like a crown. Of all the nine major species of spiral horns, my favorite to hunt is the only amphibious member of the tribe, *Tragelaphus spekii*, or as it's more commonly referred to, the Sitatunga. The challenge of pursuing these swamp dwelling beauties on their home turf, or better put, on their home mush, is second to none.

October found me and my posse, Mack Padgett (the high-tech redneck), and the infamous wonder guide, Schalk Tait, once again in Tanzania's backwoods. We had come there specifically to collect some of these rare antelope, while also attempting to whack a brace of buffalo if the gods allowed.

After a week and a half of settling in to a routine where Mack and my internal clocks adjusted to halfway around the world and letting our souls catch up to where our bodies had landed, Schalk announced at dinner one night that in the morning, early, we would be moving to a different camp, a more "rustic" basic camp, to see if we could scare up a Sitatunga. He said he had spoken on the radio to the camp manager there and that they had seen some good bull antelope and had built some *machans*. They had also patterend the Sitatungas' routine and were waiting for us to go hunting with them. Beers were clicked together in "cheers" before we strolled back to our tents to put a small bag of essentials together for the short diversion the next morning.

The high-speed, 5-hour drive to the spike camp was fairly un-eventful along the two-track dirt road winding through the scrub acacia trees and open forest. The three of us rode in the open back of the Land Cruiser, our iPods cranked up, forcing the trackers and the cook also riding in the back, to listen to three white guys singing to three different tunes at the same time, while Thomas drove and the government game scout rode in the front seat, not having to endure the ear-shattering melodies.

After plenty of bumps and coated with dust from head to toe, we finally jolted to a stop at a very beautiful setting for a basic camp located on the edge of a vast swamp interspersed with islands of dry ground and palm trees. The temperature difference between the two camps was staggering in the afternoon sun as we unpacked our bags in our private thatched rondeval. The temperature gauge in the dining area hovered at a balmy 108 degrees where we all met before going out to scout the swamp and see what the locals had set up for us.

A mile drive from camp, we parked the truck in the shade at the edge of the swamp and began our trek along a well-worn hippo trail that the giant beasts used each morning and evening when they made their way to the forested feeding areas they prefer. Our local tracker pointed to a far-off island indicating that was where we were heading. I'd sprayed myself down with a good dose of mosquito repellent before starting out and Lord Almighty, was I glad I did as the tiny terrorists descended on us in waves as we reached the halfway point to the particular island we were traveling to.

The scorching sun burned down on us relentlessly as the dry trail turned to mush before gradually becoming a deeper, water-filled trench the closer we got to what we named "Sitatunga Island." The water filling my Courteney boots actually felt refreshing in the staggering heat.

As we got to within 100 yards of the island I heard Schalk curse before he started jabbering at the local guide in Swahili. The lone acacia tree living on the 20 foot x 20 foot island could now be seen supporting a wreck of a *machan*, poorly constructed atop stilts buried in the dirt of the tiny dry refuge.

As the six of us crowded onto the small island, Schalk and I began inspecting more closely the structure we had planned perching upon. The whole contraption leaned at a 25-degree angle over the swamp, with a couple of ropes lashing it back to the acacia, the ladder missing half its rungs. Schalk glassed the other islands spread out around us and mumbled something else to the locals that didn't sound like they were being complemented on their fine workmanship.

"They say they had the blinds built 2 weeks ago, but then a storm came through last week and blew them all down except this one. When I spoke to them on the radio, they failed to mention the

This doesn't look too safe to me

storm," Schalk whispered to Mack and me. "I don't want to start rebuilding them now, because they say this is where the two big bulls were sighted. I'm not sure I believe them, but we're here so... If we make too much noise screwing with the blind, we could scare them off. Let's glass from here and see what happens since we're already here."

"Sounds good," I whispered back as I swatted at the cloud of mossies buzzing in my ears, searching for a weak spot in my chemical defenses. I turned to fill Mack in on what Schalk had whispered and saw him grinning back at me from beneath a green mosquito-proof head net, calm and comfortable.

"Dag nabbit," or something similar escaped from my lips as I realized I had left my own net back at camp. *That won't happen again.*

We glassed the surrounding swamp until dark, only seeing one small bull and half a dozen females before we silently followed the hippo trail back to the truck.

That night at dinner after a couple of cocktails, Schalk vented his frustration at the camp staff for not having the *machans* built for us, but the whole thing was quickly brought into perspective when Mack uttered the truest words ever spoken in a situation like this.

"It's Africa, what did you expect? We'll get one of these things; we always do. Anyone want a beer while I'm up?"

If there's one thing we've learned through all these years of traveling to third world countries, it's that getting yourself worked up about problems that arise constantly during the trip does absolutely no good and only exasperates the problems. You just have to stay positive and roll with the punches...and hopefully, get lucky.

The next morning after a fitful attempt at sleep in the unrelenting heat, we were back sloshing our way into the swamp an hour before dawn. There was no moon, and we didn't want to use headlamps as it might scare off the Sitatunga so the going was tough and dangerous. The sudden loud grunt and soggy crashing of a hippo 20 yards in front of us scattered our entourage in every direction as three safeties clicked off simultaneously as we all wondered which way the giant beast was coming from in the pitch-dark. It thankfully decided that escaping into the darkest corners of the morass was wiser than taking on the ponytailed Schalk Tait and his .500 Jeffrey.

Everyone soon fell back in line as some hushed nervous chatter among the trackers rebolstered our bravado. The mosquitos hadn't woken up yet when we silently crowded onto the island in the dark. Schalk tied some rope he had brought from camp onto one of the legs of the *machan* and had the trackers quietly push from the other side trying to square the legs up somewhat. The rope helped but the *machan* was still far from what one might call "safe."

Remembering the story of Mauro Daolio breaking his back and his client breaking several bones when the *machan* they were hunting from the year prior to this collapsed quickened my pulse as Schalk climbed slowly up the rickety ladder to get a better view above the 10-foot tall swamp reeds as the eastern sky began a rosy glow announcing a new day.

Mr. Tait wasn't up the ladder more than 5 minutes when he looked down with the sly smirk on his face that tells you something's going to happen real quick. He whispered, "Get ready. There are two bulls, and one of them is super, crossing an open spot. When they go behind the pile of papyrus, I'm going to climb down and you come up here and whack him."

We could not see him from our position standing under the blind because of the height of the swamp reeds surrounding it, so we had to take Schalk's word for it. While I watched him glassing, I double-checked my .375 H&H, making sure I had one up the snoot. We had not brought any light rifles on this safari, so while it may be a little bit of overkill to use a caliber of this size on a 150-pound animal, I had no choice, plus, I love the old Winchester. She's never let me down.

My guide stayed glued to his binos, searching the papyrus thickets thoroughly. Suddenly, he lowered them and slid down the ladder.

"He's the back one. There's no question which one is the big one. You'll know. Take your time. They don't know we're here."

I slung the heavy rifle over my shoulder and eased up the rickety ladder. Schalk told the trackers to lean into a corner leg of the *machan* to steady it as I climbed. The way the ladder was structured, there was no way I could get a solid rest to make the 200-yard shot that was required. I could see the papyrus island Schalk had described where the Sitatunga had apparently walked behind, but the antelope were nowhere to be seen. However, it allowed me time to fuss about on the ladder, looking for a good rest, but all to no avail. I couldn't get the shot I needed from the ladder.

With no option left but to climb up onto the rickety platform of the fragile *machan* 15 feet above the island, I eased onto the layered sticks that formed the floor, sliding forward very carefully on my belly. From down below I heard a muffled, "Uhhhh, ah ah ah, that doesn't look like a good idea," said Mack as he also grabbed a supporting leg and held it steady.

Even with everyone holding on, the *machan* was teetering with every slothlike move I made. A railing encircled the platform, and it just so happened to be at the perfect height for a rest, so I slid the Winchester over it, searching for the bulls still hidden in the reeds.

Schalk, being the mind reader that he is, climbed up a couple of rungs and tossed my backpack up to me so I could rest the butt of the rifle on it. I slipped my hat under the fore stock so it would not be resting on bare wood and was as ready as I was going to be.

As the first bull stepped out from behind the cover, the *machan* let out a moaning creak as it tipped slightly to one side. Two of the trackers switched positions to stop the contraption from falling down as I repositioned myself to get the crosshairs on the spiral-horned antelope emerging from the papyrus.

The first one wasn't bad, considering any dead Sitatunga is a good one, but I wanted to make sure and see both of them before shooting. As the first one walked slowly into thicker cover and disappeared again, the second bull quickly emerged from the papyrus and followed his tracks, loping into the same thicket. This was the one all right, a real dandy with deep curls to his twisting headgear! All I could do was wait to see where they came out and hold as steady as I could, praying the *machan* would stay together long enough for me to get a shot off.

"Here comes the smaller one," hissed Schalk perched halfway up the ladder as the first antelope cleared the tallest grass.

All I could see of him was the head and neck. The rest of his body still covered by the shorter grass, when, as if on cue, the bigger one appeared 10 feet behind his little brother. They sloshed forward, prancing like a stallion, and the grass began to thin out as I followed their progress in the scope, hoping the big one would track the little one into a shootable position.

Something—and I wasn't sure whether it would be good or bad—was about to happen when the smaller of the two ran forward 30 feet and froze. Something had gotten his attention. The big one pantomimed his buddy.

Schalk hissed, "The wind has switched. That little one smelled us. Shoot the big one now."

I followed the line of his neck down into the thin reeds, barely able to make out the density of his back. It would be a risky shot until, fortunately, the big bull took four steps forward and I could clearly make out his shoulder on his fourth step. I squeezed the trigger, and the boom of the rifle, mixed with the recoil, set the blind and me to rockin' and rollin'.

Schalk jumped down to help support a leg as I reloaded and both Sitatunga ran into a large papyrus thicket 75 yards ahead of them.

"I'm pretty sure you hit him, but you would think that .375 would have flattened him if you hit him good," Schalk said.

"The shot felt fine. I was pretty stable, but you never know," I hesitantly answered.

"Let's go see."

Off we trudged into the ankle-deep black watery muck that soon rose to our shins. One of the locals said something to Schalk, who turned to Mack and me and said, "Watch for crocs. He says there are some deep channels out here, and they are hard to see in this shit."

Great! The hippos and snakes and mossies aren't bad enough? I thought to myself.

We trudged to the spot where we had last seen the Sitatunga and one of our trackers made a little jump over a channel of open water landing shakily on the far mushy bank. Schalk stopped to look for a good crossing place, but yours truly, in my impatient excitement to find the bull, attempted a leap where the tracker had jumped. The spongy bank gave way where I began my leap. Before I could recover, I slid feetfirst up to my armpits in the stinking water.

Only the fact that I held my rifle in both my hands and it caught on the edges of the channel kept me from going in over my head. The laughter from the whole crew directed at my misfortune subsided

Did he say there are crocs in here?

as I struggled, swearing at all of them in Swahili and English, to give me a hand and get me out.

The tracker and Mack each held an end of the rifle and pulled me up onto the spongy bank, at least pretending that it wasn't that funny anymore. The rest of the crew found a drier spot to cross, and we continued on another 50 feet, me sloshing along covered in stinking swamp muck. Suddenly, to everyone's surprise, Schalk let out a whoop and yelled, "Here he is!"

We all crowded around the magnificent beast, shot through the heart, and shook hands as we admired his gorgeous long horns. We pulled him out of the water to a dry hump of matted reeds for pictures, but the spongy surface would not support us for more than a few minutes before it gave way and the water crept up our legs, quickly passing our knees. We hurriedly snapped a few trophy

Wet and covered in leeches

poses before getting to the task of skinning the animal for a life-sized mount.

I held one leg as Mack grabbed another and the boys were just about to start the skinning process when I looked down at the bloody entrance wound and saw the flesh under the hairy hide twitching and boiling with movement. Out of curiosity at the strange happening, I reached down and pushed the edge of the wound and out slid a handful of black leaches that had slithered into the body cavity through the bullet hole searching for blood.

The skin movement had been from the scores of numbers of suckers that were inside looking for a free lunch. I didn't even bother pulling my pant legs up for an inspection, knowing I would have to pry plenty of the lecherous vermin off later when we got back to dry ground. A shudder ran up my spine thinking of all possible

Leeches were everywhere as we skinned it out for a life-size mount

appendages the slimy black bastards might be latching onto, so I urged the skinners to hurry up. At this time, the mosquitoes started to harass us as well. Occasionally, I glanced over my shoulder into the channel I had just taken a dip in, wondering how big the crocs got around here.

A dandy East African Sitatunga

The Ham Slam?

IT WAS DAY 4 of a 10-day hunt in the Odo Bulu concession of the jungle-covered Bale Mountains of South-Central Ethiopia, and I was out of breath as I looked quickly across the green, vine-covered chasm separating Jason Roussos and our crew from the pig of my dreams. It was a real hog if there ever was one, with a porcine mug so ugly that even his mother couldn't love.

The 5-minute panicked run up the game trail from where we had perched glassing a gap in the jungle thicket because I did not want to be left behind by my young professional hunter had me gasping deep double breaths. My heart rate was beating at double time. It needed to get back to a level where the crosshairs would not be dancing the mambo when I settled in behind them.

A runner had urgently come to tell us that they had a Giant Forest Hog at this spot and that we needed to hurry up to this location to shoot it before it disappeared back into the jungle. Being a sea-level-dwelling city boy was taking its toll on my heaving chest, and the 7,500 foot altitude engulfing us in these Mountain Nyala-haunted crags was delaying the end of the dancing crosshair performance as well. I didn't want to blow this shot; no way, not this one. I'd come a long way to get to this point...

The first wild pig of any sort that I killed was on my first safari to Africa, to the newly named Zimbabwe, where I hunted in the Dande area with Sten Sedregren. I knew all the major species available on license, but have to admit that when the two of us were sneaking quietly through the dry river thickets, sweating like a "proverbial pig" in the late afternoon heat and Sten halted and whispered in my ear, "Do you want a bush pig?" I had no idea what they were, what they looked like, or how big they were. I really wanted to ask how much they cost since I was on a tight budget in those days, with a wife and child to feed back home, but instead, I whispered, "Sure."

Sten pointed to our right into the darkest part of the thicket where I found in the scope a big brown and black blob of hairy animals in a pile about the size of a dozen 100-pound sacks of potatoes.

So that's a pig pile, I guess, I thought before hissing to Sten, "Which one?"

"The biggest one," he sharply hissed back.

All I could make out was hair in the scope. I was barely able to discern one body from another until on the right side of the pile a bigger-than-normal chunk of potential holiday ham came into focus. I took a big chance, one I would not repeat, and shot into the pile, causing complete pork panic as the pig pile erupted into bodies of every size imaginable scattering to the wind—all except one and luckily it turned out to be the big boar of the herd who was stone-cold dead.

Many times since I've heard of fellow hunters who have superb collections of animals but are missing the elusive bush pig due to its passion for thriving nocturnally in the aptly named dense bush. Recently some folks have figured out how to successfully bait them and the kill rate has skyrocketed; before then, the success rate was dismal on the longheaded swine.

In the years since, I have continued my lucky streak with the boars from around the world. Strangely enough, the Russian boar and its evolutionary offspring have settled into almost every corner of the world, creating hunting opportunities and challenges to sportsmen everywhere. In some areas, the wild boar is at or near the top of the most-sought-after animals in its local domain.

The Germans and surrounding countries go absolutely bonkers over pigs that have been hunted now for a couple thousand years. They are perhaps the cagiest of the species. These European pigs can get huge. I was able to take a big-bodied one of over 400 pounds with Klemens Bugelnig in Austria in the forested hills above the quaint village of Puchberg.

In Central Asia, I once shot a boar at over 9,000 foot elevation while hunting Dagestan Tur in some of the steepest canyons I have ever witnessed. I couldn't believe my eyes when I saw the pig ambling along a path that would have frightened an ibex. With my guide's AK 47, I took the big boar out at 75 yards, rolling the beast all the way to the bottom of the chasm, from where it took the guides 6 hours to retrieve it.

The boar hunting in Turkey may be the best there is since the local Muslim population doesn't hunt or poach them, let alone touch them after you kill them. My biggest tusks for a wild boar came from the Adana area only 15 minutes from the thriving 5-star resort town. While regular tourists were settling down to a pleasant meal in one of the many fine restaurants, my Turk guides and I were out literally whacking and stacking pigs on a gravel road leading through the small farms.

Hawaii is quite famous for its traditional pig hunts. Sometimes trained mongrel dogs will bring the boars to bay, then the hunter will wade into the fray with a long-bladed knife, aptly referred to as a pig sticker, and thrust it into the pig's heart or spine, depending on what target is being offered to you by the melee of dogs and the pig in a moment of absolute panic. These black boars can also be hunted on any of the islands with more commonsensical weapons, and you can stalk them and not have to hassle with the frantic dogs. If you

Turkish boar

haven't done it yet, tie in a 1-day pig hunt next time you are in the islands with your family. It sure beats another day stuck by the pool.

Speaking of islands, of course there are big boars rampaging
further out into the South Pacific and Australia. New Zealand tends
to have quite a few free-ranging pigs that are not completely black
as most wild boars are, due, I would suspect, to some breeding with
domestic pigs that range in pastures. Not all the domestic pigs are
confined to pens like most commercial operations.

The body sizes in New Zealand and Australia can be staggering, once again, due to the perfect habitat, no predators, and abun-
dant food in the form of farmers' crops. Talk about pig heaven. Put
a pig in a stand of ripe corn and sit back and watch one of nature's
eating machines go to work on it and do some big-time damage. Be
glad that you are not the farmer that owns the cornfield.

New Zealand boar

In America, the feral boar, a derivative of Russian boars and domestic pigs gone wild, evolved with a changing body shape. Their front shoulders put on mass, and coarse black hair developed on their shoulders and neck.

Pigs, being highly intelligent and adaptable to virtually any habit with no fear of coexisting near humans, have become a scourge in many parts of the USA, especially to farmers in the South and Texas, where they have to be eradicated by using helicopters to thin their numbers. In other parts of the country, though, you can still stalk wild boar as well as use dogs to bring them to bay. Northern Californians treat them as a trophy animal, and rightly so, in my opinion. They are found in the oak forests and surrounding farmlands.

The fact that pigs are so adaptable was well illustrated one duck hunting day when a buddy of mine, Mike Upchurch, was out for a morning shoot on our mutual friend Dr. Perry De Loach's farm in north Georgia. He was stunned to see a huge black head swimming through the 3-foot deep flooded cornfield, munching away on the free lunch. Mike cancelled his dinner reservation with a load of number twos from his 12 gauge.

In South America, the wild Russian boar has taken over most of the continent and coexists with the three peccary brothers naturally found there, the white-lipped variety and the collared type, both very good prey and the white–lipped is a super aggressive contender not to be taken lightly. The collared peccary is also found as far north as Texas and in some of the other border states. I hunted them in Texas with Sterling Mize and Rowdy McBride on Clayton and Modesta Williams's ranch as an add-on to a free-range Aoudad sheep hunt.

Back on the African continent, a variety of pig-type prey is available on license in most countries and makes a welcome fatty addition to the larder when on safari, as the dry meat of all the antelope species gets pretty boring after day 18 when you eat the same thing over and over again for dinner. The most prolific and famous of the pig variety on the Dark Continent would have to be the warthog, with his long-pointed tusks making a superb trophy in anyone's game room.

I have no idea how many warthogs I have killed throughout the years, but it's a lot, as *in really a lot*. In many locations they are

A very good warthog

used as leopard bait. I have spent many nights trying to shoot a leopard (see the story in *Close Calls and Hunting Adventures*), and that equates to several braces per trip of pigs.

I love hunting warthogs and enjoy collecting their white over-sized choppers, even making a few curios out of them like knife handles, beer openers, and dice when I get bored back in the city and have time on my hands.

The other pig that closely resembles the aforementioned bush pig is the elusive red river hog, found in the jungles of Cameroon, Central African Republic, and other jungle-infested countries neighboring this vicinity. This species lives in the thickest, wettest, nastiest jungle environment you can find in Africa. It prefers to stay in the darkest thickets. If you want one, and by the way, very few people have collected one, you have to suck it up, get on your hands and knees, and silently track them through muck and red clay creek bottoms in temperatures and humidity that make you soon realize why so few people bother with them.

I was able to collect one while hunting with famed French PH Rudy Lubin while on my second safari in the Central African Republic. In the process of tracking the hogs for several days, we were bitten by ants, spiders, forest flies, and God knows what else, and we got close on several occasions to whacking one. But the big difficulty was that even if you do get close enough to shoot one, which means within *10 to 25 feet* due to the thickness of the jungle understory, you still have to pick out the boar from the rest of the herd that may number up to a dozen animals, all scurrying about in the morass of vegetation.

The males do not have large tusks and both the male and female have hair at the jaw where the tusks on the male should show, so glassing each adult animal for tusks as they appear, then quickly disappear in the forest, is hugely frustrating. The dead giveaway on pigs when deciding a male from a female is, of course, if you can get a view of their backside. If the animal is a male, his testicles will show clearly and you will have no doubt about his manhood.

Finally, after several humid, nasty days of sneaking around in the CAR jungle, we collected a dandy one, and I believe it gave me almost as much satisfaction as the Bongo I also collected with Rudy.

But, of the entire world's huntable swine, the best of them all—the rarest, the biggest, the Mount Everest of pig poking—is the giant forest hog. These huckster hams are found in jungle-type environments, in places not necessarily near each other as is the case of the populations in Ethiopia. This population is over 1,000 miles of savanna and desert from any other related populations.

I had hunted them in the Central African Republic for several weeks, but was not successful. You can also hunt them in Cameroon and other pockets across Africa, but typically with a very poor

Red river hog, a tough hunt

success rate. So when I was told by Jason Roussos that he had a permit to hunt one and he said, "Don't worry, I'll get you one," I was a little skeptical—until day 2 of the hunt when Jason said to me as we looked at a male hog only 175 yards away, standing broadside, "We can do better than that one."

Passing on a giant forest hog? Are you nuts, Jason? If it's a decent male, let's shoot the sonnava bitch, is what ran through the gray matter that supposedly keeps my sex drive and hunting passion in check as I looked through the scope at the brute that was all but dead if only I squeezed off a shot with my .7 mm! But he calmly convinced me we had time and that they had shot big ones in Odo Bulu before, like the Top Ten monster my buddy Bruce Keller shot there a couple years before my trip.

But returning to the hillside at the beginning of this tale, it was now finally my turn to shoot one and as my staccato breathing settled into a manageable routine I found the big boar Jason pointed out at the top of the clearing. The boar was lying on his side when I discovered him in the Swarovski scope, the rest of the group rooting around in the natural salt lick carved into the hillside by years of pig snouts rooting away at the saline. The angle was little strange for a shot and I do prefer lying down shots when possible. However,

The view from where I shot my giant forest hog

as Jason and I whispered the various options back and forth to each other, it became glaringly apparent that if the boar got up and took three steps, he would vaporize back into the jungle. I had a dead rest and my breathing was seminormal.

"I can rake one forward into him, and he's only 135 yards away," I told my young guide.

Before Jason finished the short utterance, "Take him," I squeezed the trigger. The boar staggered to his feet, walked unsteadily four steps, and then, just as I was about to give him another dose of a 165 grains of copper, he rolled onto his side and slid 5 feet down the mountain, getting caught up thankfully in the thick intertwined brush.

The remaining sow and piglet hogs milled around, not sure what had happened, until our troop on the opposing mountainside

Jason and Amy Roussos with the forest hog hunting crew

started whooping it up in celebration. That sent the herd back into the jungle to find a new sire for their sounder.

After the usual photo-taking routine, we dug out the knives and were about to get at it when Jason stood up, looking me seriously in the eye and said, "So now you have killed one of each of all the huntable pigs of the world. Congratulations."

As he shook my hand he continued, "You know you are one of the few people on earth to have taken the Ham Slam!"

I nearly fell down the mountainside laughing as I replied, "You better get that copyrighted!"

Russian Cowboys

ONE OF THE TREATS of getting to hunt in different countries around the world is being able to observe firsthand the various hunting and outfitting methods employed to make your journey to some remote camp successful. Sure, the variety of terrains, i.e., African savanna versus Alaskan tundra versus Himalayan mountains creates a diversity in gear and equipment required to meet the task, to the degree that very few items from one hunt's suitcase would show up at the other, except, of course, the always needed rain gear and binoculars. The clothes and boots required for a polar hunt have no home in the jungles of Cameroon any more than a .270 that suits the needs of a sheep hunt in Asia would do you any good when faced by an enraged jumbo in Botswana.

But some things always remain the same, like your daypack, with its basic contents of camera, toilet paper, skinning knife, sanitary wipes, lens cleaners, granola bar, and rain gear. Until my latest sheep hunt in Russia, I would have said the same was true about horse packing as well. It's pretty basic and everyone does it the same, right? Well, I stand corrected. Not everyone...

Let me state right here that I am no expert on horse wrangling, tying a diamond hitch, or controlling crazed nags, but I have been on over 30-some odd horseback trips in various nooks and crannies on earth, so I have some experience. I've also owned and cared for my share of equine flesh, and now that I do not own any, feel much

63

the same way as people who have purchased boats. That is, the two best days of owning them are the day you buy them and the day you *sell* them.

I'm reminded of a couple of notorious nags such as Old Steel, probably the fartingist nag to ever carry a human being. Then there was Denny the Wonder Horse from British Columbia. He would randomly go berserk for no apparent reason, even though he was handled and packed in expert fashion by Billy or Devlin Oestrich, his owners at Bradford and Company. They, as well as most outfitters in Canada and the western USA who utilize horses in their adventures, spend countless hours making sure loads are weighed, balanced on the horses' backs and sides, tied with some sort of secret knots (the knowledge of which is withheld from the clients who try to help), then tarped and roped around one last time.

Some wranglers take it to the extreme on how much weight and balance each horse can take. I've been in camps where the cowboy actually had a scale and weighed each bundle and poniard before settling on the perfect distribution for each horse. These are usually the same guys who will only let the horse carry a hundred pounds or so, *total*, insisting that is enough for each nag. Now when I work through the math on this and consider that my scrawny frame comes in at 160 pounds wet out of the shower, and my hunting partners, who may not be necessarily as svelte as your humble scribe, tip the scale at over 200 and will be riding a horse, why only 100 pounds on the packhorse? Sounds like a make work project for unemployed union member equines if you ask me.

One of these breed of packers was on a trip to the Yukon after Stone Sheep, where Mack Padgett (the high-tech redneck from Jacksonboro, S.C.) and I had only seen one shootable animal, which was a nice bull moose, over a 14-day miserable venture in the rugged mountains. When the beast wandered into our rain-drenched sheep camp and stood staring at us from 75 yards away, the guide would not let us shoot the moose, as we were, as he firmly put it, *"too far in the mountains. We will never get it out of here."*

I looked at the assembled horses hobbled in the foggy wet camp, looked back at the moose standing broadside, making amorous gestures toward the horses, figuring in his lust-filled frenzy that they were cow moose, I suppose, and put my rifle to my shoulder to shoot the lust-crazed moose anyway. The hell with what the guide said.

Before I pulled the trigger, however, the guide actually reached over and grabbed the barrel of my gun and lifted it up over my head so I couldn't shoot. During the ensuing "conversation" between us over, *"What are these nags here for if not to carry out meat and horns?"* and him saying that *"It would take forever as the trail is so steep and blah, blah, blah"* whining, the moose finally had enough of our shenanigans and took off for more sociable mates.

A few days later when we met up with the three other unsuccessful hunters at the main cabin, still a good 10 hours of riding from where the floatplane would pick us up, we were told that the next day we would be taking all the packhorses out of the mountains with us and closing down the camp, since we were the last group of clients for the year.

Normally, had we killed something or we had not run out of food or the guides were not idiots, this wouldn't have been that big of a deal, but by 10 the next morning when the guides and the owner of the outfit were still screwing around with all the nags and meticulously setting up each pack frame, then reweighing, then moving one poniard over to this horse and that one over here, all of us clients were fuming and starting to get somewhat belligerent. We all saddled our own horse while we waited, which got the wranglers' undies in a bunch, and, of course, they had to inspect, retie, restrap each one, even though I've done it a thousand times myself and it was perfect.

Finally the pack train of over 30 nags of various breeds and colors were assembled, lined up, tied to each other, and our procession began the slow journey to the lake with the four hunters riding at the rear of the train as instructed.

An agonizingly slow hour after we began the forced march we came to a wet, muddy area perhaps 50 yards wide and half that in length. As the train continued around the worst part, easily negotiating the mucky ankle-deep mung, the head honcho rode back to us and told us to get off the horses and lead them around the morass.

I replied, "If the packhorses can make it through, I'm sure my steed will be just fine with me on top of him."

The other fed up hunters grumbled their collective agreement with my logic, and the boss rode back to his position, silently stewing because his orders were not being followed.

At this point the trail was wide and I noticed the other side of the muck had a better trail going around it. Seizing the opportunity, I turned in the saddle toward Mack and quietly said, "You know there is a case of beer at the lake that they made us leave behind since it would be too heavy." Mack, not needing any more encouragement than the magic word *beer*, put his heels into the ribs of his horse at the same moment as I did, and we maneuvered our willing mounts at a cantor to the other side of the muddy spot where we met the main trail again. We gave the anxious horses who knew they were heading for the barn, all the rein they needed and spurred them into a full run.

The last thing I heard as we raced by the pack train owner was, "Don't run those horses. You won't be able to control them!"

By the time the pack train showed up at the lake several hours after we had, a serious dent had been put in the case of golden refreshment.

Spring forward to 2009, Bill Figge (grower of the biggest blackbucks in the world) and I are hunting in one of the former

Texas Cowboy Bill

Russian "Stans" where we are standing in a cold drizzle under gray skies, watching a crew of four Muslim erstwhile cowboys securing ancient worn leather saddles to big, strong-looking horses. These guys had no illusions about using a lead rope to tow the nags Bill and I would be riding safely behind them, like most outfitters insist on doing.

No, they were going to let us ride on our own, cowboy-style, which was fine with us. As they began to load the duffle bags, camping gear, and food, along with the pots and pans and propane tanks, on the two packhorses, it was apparent that they had never been to the Yukon Territories school of horse packing. One big black horse stood sedately by as duffle bags belonging to Bill and I were roped tightly to its sides. No special pack frame was used or needed, just an old riding saddle held the lot. On top of this were piled tarps,

How to not pack a horse

salt bags, and being that this was, after all, a former Russian colony, two cases of local vodka. The horse didn't seem to mind the load being over 250 lbs. or the fact that it was definitely heavier on the left side than the right.

The other steed, a grayish-white gelding of unknown age, was then loaded high and wide with the remaining gear. Just when I was about to interrupt the process and suggest moving a couple of the feed bags turned into duffle bags so they would ride better, Bill caught my attention and shook his head intimating, *"Don't say anything, Alain. Let them do it their way."*

He, of course, was right, and since most of the stuff on the gray was theirs, I wasn't too concerned about the consequences—until the last two remaining items were loaded on, one of them

Since everything is packed securely, I think I'll call
my wife and see what she's doing

being my last duffle bag and the other being the pots and pans. I was surprised that the horse didn't jump or start making a scene when the noisy bundle of kitchen gear was banged against his side, a rope strung haphazardly around the mess, and my bag tied to the saddle with some orange hay string on the other side of the animal.

Off we went toward the looming mountains shrouded in gray mist, the gang spread out in no semblance of order, with the two packhorses being led by one of the locals. We made it a half hour before the first bag fell off the gray horse. The guy leading it got off, loaded it back on, and resecured it with some more twine. An hour later, the mesh bag containing the pots and pans slipped underneath the horse's belly.

Dismounting, the cowboy pushed it back around to where it was to start with, then simply continued on, no extra rope or twine being applied. This happened at regular intervals over the next 7 hours as we made our way to the camp they had at the base of the Tur inhabited mountains.

Surprisingly everything made it with no breakage, even the vodka, which the guides proceeded to consume all night, giving us a late start the next morning, our first day of hunting.

The way out after a successful hunt was much the same routine, except this time, the gray packhorse decided he had had enough of the banging pots and pans when they slid under his belly on the steepest, tightest part of the muddy trail as we wove through the dense forest, a cliff of unknown height looming menacingly to our left.

When the pots and pans slipped, this time hitting the horse on the back legs hard, it sent Old Gray into a bucking bronco routine that would have made any rodeo horse proud. The panicked horse was able to shed most of his load, while knocking two of us off our mounts. I smashed into a rough-barked tree as I fell to the ground,

Sometimes it's better to walk

holding on to the pine for dear life so I wouldn't tumble over the cliff as I was sure the nag was going to buck itself to the rocky creek bottom below. It didn't, and the lead man recaptured the wild-eyed horse, got him settled down, then proceeded to pile the entire load back on him in an even more disheveled way. I offered some un-asked for advice, pulling some parachute cord out of my pack to help secure some of the stray gear, and no one seemed to mind that I butted in, probably due to their hungover state of mind.

Two more blowups with both packhorses involved in the fi-ascos happened before we finally made it back to the village we had originally departed from. Bill and I arrived relatively unscathed after we had held on for dear life for the last half hour as our trusty steeds decided they were ready for the barn, broke into a full gal-lop over the rough ground, huffing and blowing as if they were

A fine load of horns and meat

Secretariat followed by Bold Ruler coming around the clubhouse turn racing for the finish line.

Yep, people do things differently in divergent parts of the world, but in this case, perhaps the mountain cowboys of the Yukon have a better technique and could teach our Russian caballeros a thing or two. There has to be a happy medium in there somewhere. Maybe some sort of cowboy exchange program? I'll mention it to my congressman next time I see him...

Snakes

IT HAD BEEN A restless night; the mice that decided to have a shindig celebrating some vermin holiday in the thatched roof of our rondeval had kept us up most of the night with their shenanigans. You would have thought that the liquor mixed with jet lag might have had us sleeping like Grant in his tomb, but no, the mouse dance party prevailed. I threw my shoe at them once around two in the morning, which only seemed to change the tempo from a waltz to the Charleston. Mack uttered a few simple phrases regarding their mice parentage as he pulled his pillow over his head, trying to dull the noise of the critters running about in the dry grass thatching of the ceiling. The five A.M. wake-up call came what seemed like only 15 minutes after I had finally fallen asleep.

After a grueling morning of climbing around the hills and rocky valleys of Natal, South Africa, we drove back to the old lodge where we were staying at to wolf down some lunch.

Mauro Daolio, our professional hunter, suggested after some wine and a fabulous meal complete with fresh made pasta (after all, with a name like Mauro you better know how to make great pasta, capiche?) that Mack and I sit out in the afternoon at a spot he knew overlooking the Mkuze River, where he was positive lots of different species of antelope and perhaps a Natal Red duiker would come to water in the heat of the day.

He dropped us off with an ice chest filled with ice and liquid refreshment designed to keep us amused while he and the staff went about their chores for the afternoon. I was honored that our trusty PH would leave us to fend for ourselves and select the trophy animals that would surely flock to the waterhole in droves. I knew he'd be proud of us when he returned and we had killed a couple of incredible species that would surely make the Top Ten of the Safari Club International record book.

Wisely, no other guide in his right mind who has had to babysit us in the past would dare leave Mack and me alone with bullets and guns and an abundance of targets available, unsupervised, but this was our first adventure with Mauro, so he didn't know any better.

We settled into the lawn chairs strategically placed under a shady acacia tree on the lofty edge of a hundred foot high cliff with a great view of the opposite sandy shoreline, centered the ice chest between us, and watched the Land Rover drive away.

We both proceeded to fall asleep in less than two minutes...

I distinctly remember waking to the rustling of leaves under my aluminum lawn chair and wondering what I had done to the venerated mouse gods to piss them off so badly that they wouldn't even let me have a nap in peace without disturbing it.

I kept my eyes closed for another 5 minutes, begging the Lord above for a little sympathy, but finally gave up as the crescendo of my hunting partner's snoring harmonized with the crunch of leaf litter around my chair. I have to admit that I sometimes have a short fuse on my temper, and the fuse was burnt very close at this point to the dynamite that is my revenge against the disturbers of my sleep.

With my blurry eyes beginning to focus on the noise in the dry brown leaves between the chairs, I noticed for the first time movement. Seeing no black or brown pelage of a mouse, I figured the little bastards must be in among the leaves doing whatever they do to irritate mankind.

As if my sight had suddenly become crystal clear, the natural camouflage pattern of the leaves gave way to three-dimensional reality, and I made out the distinct rectangular pattern of python skin, which immediately turned out to be attached to a live, breathing python, as round in diameter as a grapefruit, and whose length was beyond my line of sight.

Since Mack and I have a symbiotic relationship due to innumerable hours in the bush together, that gives us moments of united clairvoyance, I was not surprised when his snoring abruptly ended and he glanced out of the corner of his sleep-deprived eyes to see what was up. I'm sure that the fact that I was as white as a ghost exuding fear, that I was soaking wet with nervous sweat, and that I was frozen in place like a statue of Lord Delamore waiting for a pigeon, staring at the ground to my right had him worried. I moved only me eyes upward to meet his, then motioned with them downward to where Mr. No Shoulders lay, then back up to meet Mack's gaze and mouthed the word, "Snake."

Mack, still groggy from the wine and lunch, questioned what I whispered, but followed my line of sight to the leafy ground. Looking back, I think it took him 3 or 4 seconds to realize exactly what he was looking at 1 foot away from his chair. Then in a voice that would have sounded at home on a fourth-grade girl's schoolyard, he screamed at the top of his lungs, "SNAAAAKKKKE!"

I'm not sure which one of us jumped further out of our chairs, but I can tell you he scared the holy hell out of the damn snake, which launched itself up into the air away from us toward the cliff. It was the biggest snake I had ever seen in the wild. This was a rock python, well over 12 feet long, that coiled in defense for a second after its initial leap before springing back into action and launching itself out into open air beyond the cliff.

Since we were both standing 20 feet away at this point wishing we would have grabbed our guns in our panic, we ran over to the edge to see where the snake had landed, assuming it had hit the water below. Much to our surprise and relief, we saw the great reptile wrapped securely in a tree growing out from the cliff 50 feet below.

"You'd think the fall would have killed the damn thing, eh?" I asked Mack.

"Or at least the sudden stop when it hit the tree," he quipped.

As if on cue, the snake gathered himself and slithered around the branches and worked his way on to the cliff face, disappearing from our view.

As we turned back to the tipped over chairs, Mack opened the lid to the ice chest and muttered, "Anybody else want a beer?"

~2~

Of all the snakes that slither about in this world there are none that bring on the same ancestral fear that black mambas do. A thinly built snake rarely as round in circumference as the handle of a baseball bat, they are long and built for speed. The longest one I've measured (dead, I might add) was over 13 feet, *and he was missing the front foot and a half of his body that I had blown to pieces!*

When they are hunting, they travel with the front third of their body upright, searching for prey, so you might end up looking into the reptile's eyes at 4 feet off the ground. You could assume he's looking squarely at your jugular vein, unless you are Gary Coleman, in which case he's looking over your head.

Oh, and the mamba is one of the fastest snakes on earth, so you can't even run away from him if he sets his mind on biting you.

The bite from a mamba, while not always fatal, typically is unless you are near a hospital with antivenom at the ready. Most people who survive the venom wish they hadn't. The long-term damage to flesh and muscle, not to mention internal organ destruction, leaves survivors permanently crippled. I'm not sure about God's overall plan for all his species that he placed on earth, but I can not, for the life of me, figure out the reasoning for putting such a perfect killing machine among us heathens.

The big fear of mambas among professional hunters and trackers seems to be more about when you are riding in the truck than

A big mamba white-side up

when you are walking on terra firma. A snake's natural reaction to sensing someone walking toward them is to get away, avoid confrontation, but if you are driving down a dirt track minding your own business and the driver's not paying attention and runs over a mamba's tail, you have reptile-dom's most vicious member mad as hell and able to strike multiple times faster than Mike Tyson's jabs.

Guides talk about having their mirrors struck by an enraged snake, of mambas ending up in the back of the truck after striking and missing their target, their body weight and the sheer force of their strike launching them into a quickly emptying cargo area.

Our Tanzanian driver Thomas told us about the time a huge black mamba struck his half-opened window, leaving a smear of venom at eye level on the glass. Since that day, he always drives with the window rolled up tight.

The other strange thing I find about black mambas is I've never seen a small one. I have seen (make that killed) a half-dozen mambas, and all of them were over 10 feet long. Wouldn't you think you would see say a 6-footer somewhere in your travels? Do they hide until they get big enough? I have killed all of them with a shotgun, which makes hitting the skinny reptiles much easier than trying it with a rifle.

I once saw our illustrious guide and professional hunter Schalk Tait kill a monster black mamba by throwing a shovel at the grayish mass as it tried to climb into a bush for a better look at us. He held the shovel by the handle and threw the spade from 20 feet away so it flew through the air as if it were a spear, cleanly lopping the head off the snake 4 inches below the jawline.

Looking through the foot tall grass, Schalk found the head, and we pried the fangs out from the recess in the Mamba's jaw with my handmade knife I bought in Alaska years ago, to investigate how long they were. Needlelike, with barbs a quarter way

Schalk with the shovel killed mamba missing the business end...

up them to gain a permanent hold on its victims, the fangs in the severed head's mouth began pumping venom onto the blade of the knife.

To put this whole toxic, poisonous venom stuff in perspective, imagine this. *The liquid from the fangs permanently stained the steel blade of my knife with an iridescent pattern that, after 15-plus years, has never come off.*

Mamba in a tree

How's that for potent?

Even with the head severed, the body still squirmed and twitched for 45 minutes afterward, giving our adolescent humor time to tease the trackers and game scout with the carcass, playing a few sick jokes on each other because, *"Everybody's a comedian when he's got a dead snake to play with."*

~3~

While the shovel toss by Schalk Tait ranks number one as the best Non-conventional Snake Kill ever, first place in the High-Caliber Rifle Shot Without a Rest category has to go to Piet Stein.

The South African PH was guiding my friend Mexican businessman José Antonio Rivero and his son Pedro on a full-bag safari in the Kigosi region of Tanzania. On this particular day, I was

José with black spitting cobra

invited to join them to see if we could find an East African kudu for me and an eland for José.

After a long day of glassing and driving, we decided to get out and walk into a korongo where Piet knew kudu usually hung out at this time of the day. The late-season grass was only knee high, having just started to sprout now that the rains had begun. We all got in line behind Piet in usual safari hunting mode and hadn't walked a hundred yards when movement 10 yards to our left made us all swing toward it.

Up out of the grass rose the scariest, meanest-looking snake I'd ever laid eyes on. Black as coal, as big around as a Coke can with bright orange bars reverberating across the flared-out hood, a black spitting cobra tested the air with its flicking tongue.

As José and I instinctively took a step back, raising our rifles just in case, the snake wove and danced, getting ready to let fly a dose of poison destined to blind whoever's eyes it hit. Not today though. Piet leveled his .375 at the base of the neck and fired offhand, killing the cobra instantly, much to his clients' unfettered gratitude. High fives abounded, and a few pats on the back for Piet. We took some pictures of the beady-eyed, disgustingly scary-looking reptile and headed back to the truck, watching the ground ahead at every step. No one really seemed that interested in walking to the korongo after that, so we drove around in silence until dusk forced us back to camp.

~4~

The Central African Republic can certainly put together a starting team of its own dangerous snakes, home field advantage going to the spitting cobra, black and green mamba, Gaboon viper, puff adder, and, of course, the mighty pythons, to name just a few of the star-studded lineup.

Perhaps the strangest, while not the most dangerous, encounter Mack and I have ever had with a snake happened in the CAR in 2006 while out tracking Lord Derby's giant eland in the forests of the rolling hills of the vast, virtually uninhabited country. The temperature hovered near a hundred, but the humidity was low at this time of year and we'd been on a hot track most of the afternoon.

Hunting this majestic animal the old-fashioned way—by tracking and listening as you go for the sounds of the herd breaking the high branches off the Isoberlinio trees with their towering spiral horns so they can reach the tender leaves and hearing the ethereal rumbles and grunts the antelope use to keep in contact with each other as they wander about in fair-sized herds—is as real of hunting as there is still left on the African continent.

Our entourage, led by the legendary Rudy Lubin, eventually ended back at a two-track dirt road that our PH had carved through the forest many years before. The eland had continued across it and the tracks clearly showed that the antelope were now moving fast, scuff marks in the red sandy soil revealed the whole herd had taken flight, the wind having done a 180 on us and blown the scent of three white guys and three local Banda natives straight at them.

Rudy tipped his signature green felt fedora back on his head and whispered in French-accented English, "They are gone. We will not catch them today." He looked at his watch, then up at the sun low on the horizon and continued. "Let's head back to the truck. We may make it before dark, if we hurry."

Now when Rudy says *hurry*, you better have your boots laced up tight and your hat glued on. His days of fighting in the French army and 30-plus years in the bush have made him a walking machine. It may not be mountain climbing at 15,000 foot elevation in the Himalayas, but the mean pace he sets keeps me at a half run the whole time just trying to keep up.

After 10 minutes of this blistering pace, I noticed something shiny in the middle of the road 30 yards ahead of us. Rudy was concentrating on something else, perhaps a Frenchman's lusty thoughts after being in the jungle for several months, but whatever it was I broke his thought pattern when I grabbed his sleeve and pointed at it.

As we continued closer to what appeared to be a log lying across the road, the thing moved! Holy monkeys! We were not expecting that I can tell you as we both took a step back and the rest of our entourage came up behind us.

The "log" turned out to be a tremendous python, well over 15 feet long, catching the last rays of sunshine, enjoying the warmth of the open sandy road. When we snuck closer, we saw that something wasn't quite right about this serpent monster. Its body was terribly misshapen near the head.

On closer inspection (from 10 feet away...), it turned out that the swollen north end of the snake was caused by the giant serpent having swallowed a small duiker, either of the Western or red-flanked variety that call this area home—whole! The snake didn't like us disturbing his nap one bit, hissing a hideous warning at us, swinging its football-sized head back and forth, the devilish tongue flicking in and out, testing the evening air.

The snake kept the rest of its body still even as Mack and I adolescently approached closer, curiosity getting the better of us. The rest of our troop remained a safe distance away. A shudder ran up my soul when I got to within 5 feet of the snake and saw the area where the 10-pound duiker occupied the snake's body *moving*. I could make out the tiny horns and head of the duiker, distinct from the hump-backed body as the tiny antelope made a last-ditch struggling effort at life.

A laugh from behind me took my attention away from the beast as I backed away a few feet. Rudy translated what the jabbering trackers were cackling about.

Python full of duiker

"They say, Patron, it is a '"two for one' this snake."

"What do you mean, Rudy?" I replied.

"If we kill the snake, they get duiker and python meat for dinner tonight."

Having spent a great deal of time in Africa and watched the locals' dietary habits up close, I had no doubt that Rudy was not kidding about this snake's future. A thought crossed my mind that maybe we could even save the little antelope if we hurried, but common sense said his body had been crushed to a pulp before he was swallowed headfirst, which made it even more wondrous that he was still kicking inside.

"Are we going to kill it?" Mack asked.

"No. I do not like to kill the pythons. They are good snakes, eating lots of rodents and other pests, although apparently the occasional duiker as well. I try to teach these guys to leave them alone, but when I'm not around, I'm sure they go back to their old ways of killing and eating anything they can."

I could see the disappointment all over the trackers' faces as they got the drift of Rudy's comments.

The lethargic snake had still not moved its body at all, only the head, the long, thin tongue flicking in and out, tasting the air, and it seemed as if due to the large meal filling his gullet he was not going to go anywhere soon. Knowing how much my friend hates snakes and because Mack and I feed off each other's boyish bravado, it didn't faze him when I said, "Mack, grab his tail, and I'll get a picture of it. That snake can't hardly move, and it's not poisonous anyhow, even if he bites you."

Rudy laughed and translated to the trackers, who joined in the chuckling until Mack walked around to the rear end of the python, approaching it *very* carefully. The trackers' laughter quickly turned to dread as Mack crept up behind the giant, inching closer as the snake made a futile attempt to turn and see what he was up to.

Mack about to grab the snake's tail

Seeing I had the camera ready, my hunting partner quickly grabbed the snake by the tail, giving it a pull for good measure. The hissing reverberating from the python rose two octaves as it struggled to turn on its adversary, frustrated that it could not spin with its typical lightning speed and strike out at the sassy Southern white man.

"You better be careful, Mack. The boys say the snake can bite from both ends," Rudy laughed.

"Whaaat?"

"The big pythons have two sharp bones forming a 'V' by their anal vent that they use for gripping bark when they climb up trees, and they are sharp as hell, so be careful at the end of the snake."

Of course, I was cracking up at the whole thing, snapping pictures of Mack and the shiny snake, hoping for a good shot, because I knew no one was going to believe this stuff back home. All this commotion eventually was simply too much for the overgrown reptile so it began an attempt to escape by slithering its huge form away from Mack, directly at me. Since I didn't see any reason for a picture of me anywhere near a snake, I jumped out of the way and let it pass.

Rudy said, "Aha, see the hole at the base of that anthill behind you? I bet you that's where he's headed."

Sure enough, he pushed and pulled his gorged torso to the large warthog hole, slowly disappearing into it.

Our curiosity satiated, we continued on our way quickly walking toward the truck, the sun almost finished illuminating another African day. Rudy turned his head back to me while still maintaining his blistering pace, sadness in his voice as he said, "It is too bad we are so close to camp, maybe 3 miles is all. Now that the locals know where the python lives, and they know she won't move for a week as she digests her meal, they will surely go back and kill her."

I didn't reply as I hurried on behind Rudy. I just thought, *It is Africa…*

"Very Superstitious"

This chapter is a series of recollections I have from experiences in the bush with different peoples and their beliefs and superstitions. I am not here to judge anyone's beliefs any more than I am here to change their ways. I do find it fascinating, however, to reflect on how superstitions affect people's daily lives.

SETTING UP CAMP FOR the night after the long steep climb into Nepal's Himalayan Mountains was a very welcome break. My hunting partner on this adventure was Don Snyder, one of the great sheep hunters of the world and a member of the elite "700 Club," that miniscule group of hunters who have taken the four different North American wild sheep with a total score of over 700 points. Neither of us had been to Nepal before, so the excitement of finally getting a chance to be hunting in this classic hunting environment had us antsy to start seeing some Himalayan blue sheep rams.

After the tents were set up, the pots and pans put to work on the portable stove, and water set to boil for tea, we were both summoned to the edge of camp by the head honcho, Deepak Rena, a Katmandu businessman who also owns and operates a hunting company in Nepal.

"Gentleman, the porters and the local shaman want to have a quick ceremony to bless the rifles and the hunt. Would you mind bringing your rifles over to me from your tent and make sure they are unloaded, please."

"OK," we both replied, sneaking a look at each other in wonderment of what the hell this was all about.

Emerging from my tent I saw Don standing in front of his tent, staring at the group of some 29 porters and camp staff all gathered around a scraggly tree, sitting on their haunches or any convenient rock, waiting for the action to begin.

Walking downhill to where Deepak waited, we handed our trusty weapons to the headman, who then leaned them reverently against the tree trunk where a vase full of burning incense sent a plume of spicy vapors into the thin mountain air.

The local priest, or shaman as they are called here, came forward, dressed similarly to the other men in shabby camo pants, a

The shaman blessing our rifles

button-up light green shirt, but with the added accoutrement of a flashy chrome watch.

While not exactly in full regalia as the shaman we had seen on the streets of Kathmandu had been attired, the man still carried himself as if he were outfitted in Nepalese priestly dogma.

Deepak leaned over to the two of us who stood just to the right of the tree, watching with rapt attention at the ceremony that was about to unfold and whispered, "First he will crack an egg into the vessel to read the signs in the yoke. Please remove your hats." We did as instructed and watched with rapped attention as the egg was broken into the tin pie plate that served in this instance as the "holy vessel."

Good job, I thought to myself as the egg came out of the shell perfectly, yoke intact and ready to be slapped into a frying pan with some sizzling bacon as far as I was concerned. No one said a word as the shaman wandered aimlessly about in front of the tree chanting as he closely examined the yoke. He suddenly raised the pie tin up to chin level, chanted more loudly, then turned and set the pan down on a flat rock in front of the rifles. The crowd all looked at each other, nodding in recognition of something that the priest had muttered.

"The egg is good," whispered Deepak.

A porter, who had now become a pseudoaltar boy, came forward from the crowd with a live white chicken, squawking and carrying on as chickens, whose time on earth is about to end, often do. Holding the hen over the sacred pie tin, the shaman pulled out his 14-inch Gurkha army knife, the kind that curve the wrong way, and gently nicked the chicken's neck and let the dark red blood drizzle into the vessel, while drawing some symbols in the pan with the blood. The chicken was then tethered upside down to a branch on the rifle tree by the priest's assistant as the holy man began pacing about once again with the pan held reverently in front of him as he examined its sticky contents.

Walking back to the smoke of the incense, he moved the pan in circles through the rising vapors, chanting for all he was worth as the crowd sat in rapt attention. I snuck a look over at Don, who gave me a raised eyebrow response of, "What the hell is this all about?" The holy man turned to the crowd and apparently let everyone know that stage two was perfect as everyone smiled after his pronouncement to the assembled parishioners.

The mountain blessing began to take on a whole new twist as a small brown and white goat was brought forward out of the crowd on a twine leash. We had bought the goat for a couple of bucks from some herders we met halfway up the hill earlier in the day. I can tell you in all honesty that neither Don nor I had any idea that the goat's destiny would be in a religious ceremony later in the day when we bought him and am quite sure the goat didn't realize it either...

More chanting and serious mumbo jumbo accompanied the kid goat's entrance into the makeshift altar area around the tree. The shaman now retrieved the holy vessel containing blood and egg from the rock and set it on the ground in front of the goat as if the kid was expected to drink the concoction.

The goat struggled at the tether as the spirits were called upon by the priest, who, in a flash, whipped out his long odd-shaped knife once again and in one firm slashing stroke, chopped the goat's head clean off his body. The head tumbled to the side like an oblong ball, the lips still moving while the dark brown eyes continued to blink, the brain not realizing yet that it did not have a body attached to it anymore.

The altar boy held the body upright as arterial blood from the goat pumped into the sacred pie tin. The shaman pulled the pan away once the required amount of ruby liquid had been drained and began swirling the mixture to and fro as he strolled among the enthralled believers. The goat's body finally quit twitching, and the young man let it rest peacefully on the ground in front of the now sacred tree.

Using the tip of his knife, the shaman now began stirring the mixture in the pan as the ceremony rose to a crescendo, everyone excited to know if the hunt would be a success or not, all based on what the egg and blood told the high priest. By now, Don had a different pallor about him. In fact, even the term "pale" could be used to describe his countenance, and I'm sure I had lost some color from my face as well.

Now the shaman held the pan high above his head and loudly proclaimed something to the crowd that made them all nod in positive recognition and smile broadly.

"Good sign; all is well and the hunt will be good, the rifles will shoot straight," said Deepak in a relieved voice. The shaman now

Don Snyder receiving the blessing of egg and blood

walked over to our rifles and sprinkled some of the holy mixture on the stocks before turning to us.

"Bow your heads. He will give you the sign on your forehead, now."

We did as instructed and each received a bloody mark between the eyes which made all of the porters happy and completed the ceremony. Don and I looked at each other not know how long to leave the sticky substance on and hoping it wouldn't be for the next 3 weeks, but the magic must have worked since we both eventually got our animals.

Then There's Africa...

This article came from The Star, *Johannesburg, South Africa, April 30, 1997.*

Nature Conservation called in to hunt East Cape "monster."

Bisho-Transkei villagers' complaint about a monster that is said to suck the blood and brains from its human victims was discussed in the Eastern Cape legislature yesterday.

Agriculture and Land Affairs MEC Ezra Sigwela raised the issue for the attention of the house, saying the "half fish, half horse monster" was believed to have killed at least seven people trying to cross the Mzintlava River near Mount Ayliff.

Fearful villagers told Sigwela about the monster after his Freedom Day address and demanded that something be done about the beast. The MEC said he believed the story because he had been told of the monster by a prominent community leader.

Kokstad freelance journalist Andie Nomabhunga said he received numerous reports about the monster. He said he knew of nine people who had been killed since January. The latest victim was a schoolgirl who was buried last month, he said.

Sigwela promised to ask the National Agriculture ministry to send nature conservation officers to hunt the creature.

And this article regarding the same monster from the Cape Argus newspaper, Cape Town, S. Africa. May 16, 1997.

Mamlambo on the Loose

Nine people are reported dead in South Africa's Eastern Cape Province, all said to be victims of Mamlambo, the river monster.

Most recently the giant reptile was sighted near Lubaleko, a village on the Mzintlava River not far from Mount Ayliff, about 176 kilometers southeast of Durban.

"Like many rural villages in what used to be the Transkei, Lubaleko is scattered over several square kilometers of undulating hillside country. The houses, some made of brick and others of mud, are far apart and linked only by winding footpaths. There is no electricity or piped water."

Police say the victims were drowned in the Mzintlava, which was swollen by heavy rains in Lesotho during the wet season.

"I have seen some of the bodies of the so-called monster's victims," Captain G. Mzuko of the Mount Ayliff Police told [the Cape Argus]. "They had all been in the water for some time and, as is often the case, river crabs had eaten away the soft parts of the faces and throats. In one case, the

crabs were still clinging to the body when it was brought in. As far as we are concerned, these were cases of drowning, plain and simple."

"But to the people of the village, the mutilation just proves the monster's existence. It eats their faces off and sucks out the people's brains," said an elderly Mr. Matshunga, walking the lonely track with his dogs. "It is a big snake, and I have seen what it does." Witnesses describe Mamlambo as being about 20 meters [67 feet] long, with short stumpy legs, a crocodilian body, plus the head and neck of a snake, and it shines at night with a green light."

A group of women returning from a meeting at the village school assured [Cape Argus reporter David Biggs] that the monster was real.

"We are not just ignorant, superstitious people," they told me. "We are teachers. Educated and we know that the monster is there. That is why we do not cross the river anymore."

"Mthokozisi Sigcobeka [age 6] says his father was eaten by the monster. When he is older, he plans to get a gun and hunt it."

Mamlambo is classic African superstition. You can't make this stuff up...

Witchdoctors

The following story is true and was told to me by the man involved, John Dlamini, whose original Ndebele birthright name was Machena Tshuma. However, he changed it because it sounded "cooler." Since John was Mauro Daolio and Schalk Tait's head tracker, handyman, mechanic, skinner, and all-around hard worker, and if you have read any of my past tales, you should recognize their names. You would certainly know that I hunted with John innumerable times.

John was from the Ndebele tribe in Southern Zimbabwe, or Rhodesia as it was called when John was born. John was educated in a proper school as a youngster, spoke several languages, including Afrikaans, Italian, English, Swahili, and several native tongues. His father was a politician of some sort; however, John, like many of us, preferred the bush to the big city and made his livelihood in the adventures of Zambia, Tanzania, Zimbabwe, and South Africa.

John returned home from the safari season in Tanzania with a pocket full of cash. The season had been good with many return clients who all took good care of the staff with decent tips at the end of each safari. Return clients were nice to work with since you didn't have to retrain them, and you also had the advantage of knowing from past experience what they could and could not handle when it came to long treks through the bush. John felt good; it had been a successful season—that is, until he returned home to his wife and family in Johannesburg.

John and his wife wanted to have another baby, one more child. Another son for John to go along with the other four siblings would be just right. They had no trouble with the first four, but now, it seemed his wife could not conceive any more, no matter how hard they tried.

On top of that, the children were a handful, his parents-in-law were sticking their noses in his business, and the house was not his home. To John and his wife, it appeared that someone had put a curse on him. It was plain to see that a bad spirit had been let loose in his house, and the only way to eliminate it was to find out who had put the curse on them and get them to recant it or put a stronger curse on the culprit, thereby eliminating the problem.

The local witchdoctor in John's Joberg neighborhood was known to all as a very powerful shaman, a man with godlike powers who was capable of superhuman feats—for the right price. When John went to meet with the charlatan, it didn't take long for him to pry out of John where he had been working and that John had financially been blessed quite recently. John, being a bit of a braggart, didn't help his cause at this point one bit either...

The witchdoctor closed his eyes after darkness had enveloped the main room of John's home, feeling the spirits and the curse that emanated from every nook and cranny of the Dlamini simple house. He spoke in whispers at times, at other moments, he shouted at the top of his lungs, questioning the spirits, cursing them, and begging them to move from John's family home and leave them in peace.

After a good half hour of incantations in front of an awestruck John, the witchdoctor sat back on his haunches, shaking his head from side to side, mumbling, "This is a bad curse; very bad. You must find out who caused this, and then you can get the bad spirits out of your home and your life."

"Yes," cried John, "tell me who it is; tell me, please, I beg you!"

"I can. I have the power, but you must pay me so I can appease my spirits and satisfy my helpers in the other world. John, our ancestors are watching us. Can you feel them? Do you want to make the ancestors happy? They will help us."

"Yes, yes, of course, I do!" John shouted.

"The spirits ask for a heavy price; 3,000 rand is what they seek to rid this home of the curse."

John was stunned by the cost. It was all the money he had from his wages for the hunting season, but what could he do? This was a powerful witchdoctor, and he must be able to help him. John forked over the money to the harlot, receiving for his hard earned money the following prescription:

"John, here is what you must do. First, go to the store and buy a new basin and a mirror that will fit inside the basin. Bring the basin home and fill it with water. Then put the mirror with the reflective side facing down, in the bottom of the basin. Place the basin on a table next to your bed and sleep there next to it for one night. In the morning when you wake, you are to take the basin outside in the sunlight and remove the mirror from the water. When you look into the mirror, it will show you who has put the curse on your house."

The witchdoctor then left John's house in his shiny black Mercedes, rushing off to another appointment.

John followed the instructions to a tee, and you can imagine the results...

When he went back to the witchdoctor to tell him the results and get his money back, he was harangued and bullied by the shyster and told the problem was he did not believe enough, which was his problem. He was instructed to go back and try it again.

Mauro and Schalk, of course, never let poor John live it down, telling him what he saw in the mirror was, "The baboon who gave away all his money—not the person who gave him the curse."

Another Classic John Story Follows

Mack and I had finally made it back to Africa and were excited, to put it mildly, that we were going on our first elephant hunt in Zimbabwe. My most vivid recollection of the beginning of the hunt was the heat, the staggering heat just before the rains. Even at night, the temperatures never dropped below 100 degrees. We were staying in a basic thatched hut-style camp in the southeast corner of the country, located on the Save River. There was no air conditioning, of course, or electricity, except for the small generator that was turned on during dinner for some light at the table.

We had hunted with John as our tracker in the past and really enjoyed his company and work ethic, so thought it only appropriate to bring him some presents. Among other basic items, we brought him a set of safari clothes emblazoned with the Team Pabst logo (for the uninitiated, that is Mack's and my moniker for which we are known throughout many uncivilized reaches) and a matching hat, so he would fit in with the rest of us.

John, as well as most of the trackers and camp staff we have encountered in Africa, has been known to smoke the Mbangi whenever he gets a break in the action. Now, John always had a great sense of humor, but when he got lit up on local grown marijuana, he became off-the-scale funny.

While not condoning the practice and having avoided the vice (I have plenty of others), I still thought it would be a treat for John if I brought him over some Zig Zag rolling papers from America, since I had only seen him rolling his pot up in newspaper or brown paper bag strips.

A couple of days later after a marathon trek (where we discovered that a half-dozen bulls whose ivory we found out didn't meet our picky high standards at the time), we were all taking a break in the shade of an ancient marula tree. While we finished our lunch and passed around the water jug, I glanced over and saw John rolling a Bob Marley-approved giant joint in newspaper.

"Hey, John," I said. "Why aren't you using the papers I brought you from America?"

"Ah, thank you, Bwana Alain, but you see, I use the newspaper to roll the Mbangi in. That way when I smoke it, the news from the paper goes into my brain. I use the English language newspaper, and that is how I learned to speak English also, you know."

I laughed so hard I literally started crying.

John Dlamini is not with us anymore. Unfortunately, he, like so many Africans, died of AIDS and a combination of other ailments picked up while working in the bush of Tanzania, South Africa, and Zimbabwe. I have never been around any man that could work so hard, track so well, and face danger the way John did. The only

John Dlamini and Schalk with another elephant

thing he feared was snakes, and that was another thing we had in common.

I miss John, and I still turn to see if he's next to me even today, especially when I am crawling through a thicket, scared to death that some beast is going to rearrange my scrawny physique while on safari in Africa.

We all have our strange traditions.

To put this story in perspective, I was listening to the African trackers and Thomas, our driver, chatting away about some strange voodoo experiences they had witnessed, like the man who was cursed in the local Venda village. He was cured, when according to Peter, our Christian tracker, the local witch doctor cast a demonic ridding spell upon him, at which point the man vomited up a live cow from his stomach...and was cured.

They told about vulture heads being very powerful mojo, burning of spices and certain leaves curing all sorts of ills, and being part of the witch doctor's bag of tricks. I laughed along with Mauro, the professional hunter, at the absurdity of some of the Africans' traditions—until Thomas brought up a pretty valid point about strange traditions.

"It is much like the church the Catholics have in your countries. You know what I mean? Like what is the purpose of the old man walking down the aisle of the cathedral wearing the funny pointed hat, swinging a pot on a chain that smokes, and chanting in an ancient language that no one understands?

"I do not understand why you people have the man called Jesus nailed to a cross, looking down on you in your churches either. Should it not be a happy place to go?

"Also, why do you people eat the body of your Jesus and drink his blood from a silver cup every Sunday? You people do some very strange things."

Amen, and to each his own, I suppose.

Buffalo Herders

IT'S NO SECRET THAT I believe hunting Cape buffalo is the most fun you can have, with your pants on. The fall of 2008 found the usual cast of characters that you have come to know and love namely Mack Padgett and Schalk Tait back in the Mecca of Cape buffalo, Tanzania. Joining us on their first safari to the Dark Continent were two muy machos from Mexico, José Antonio Rivero and his son Pedro. I had spent some time hunting with José in the past, but Pedro was a new addition to our entourage and I felt somewhat sorry for him. You see, we don't exactly hunt or hang out like normal people...

The buffalo in the Kigosi concession where we had decided to hunt are a breed unto their own. I don't mean that they are separate species; I mean they seem to act differently than other buff in Africa; they seem wilder, more nervous, and more unpredictable, probably due to the relentless pressure that is put on them by poachers and lions.

These huge herds of buffalo move freely between the Moyowosi and Kigosi hunting concessions and cross the Malagarasi River and adjoining swamp whenever they feel the whim to do so or as hunting pressure forces them too. I guess we got lucky because when we were in Kigosi, the buff were hanging out on our side of the swamp. Herds of hundreds of the black bovines, although mainly cows and calves, were easily found every day.

José and Pedro were being guided by South African PH Piet Stein, an experienced hand in the territory and someone who knows his buffalo. On day 2 of their first safari, both José and Pedro shot their first buffalo in a bloody tale of misfiring rifles, beasts that wouldn't stay down, and one nasty black Mbogo that decided to take a run at them, only to be dispatched by José's coolheaded brain shot with his trusty double .470 Nitro.

To make the day complete, it just so happened to be José's birthday., which one of his birthdays doesn't matter, 'cause he felt like he was 21 all over again after killing his first buff! We broke young Pedro in on how you celebrate your first buffalo kill, with beers, fine liquor, and cigars around the roaring campfire. Then the staff decided to liven things up with a decorated birthday cake, followed by some banging on pots and pans, accompanied by the trackers and kitchen staff chanting and doing native dancing. Soon, we all joined the fray, dancing the dance of drunken white guys and making up our own new Tanzanian disco favorite, "The Buffalo Dance."

Mack and I were intent on collecting some of the odds and ends species that also inhabit the Kigosi area, but decided on day 5

José with his first Mbogo

that it was time to quit screwing around with civet cat, side-striped jackals, and honey badgers and get back to some good 'ol Cape buffalo killing.

Schalk, always willing to accommodate when asked about buff hunting (I think he likes it even more than we do), came up with a plan for the next day. However, "the next day," like so many hunting days, did not go as planned. Instead, this was going to be "one of those days."

We tried everything to get up on the buffalo herds, but nothing was going right. The wind switched one time on us, sending the panicked herd hightailing back into the thick stuff; we got close to another herd, only to find out there wasn't a shooter in the bunch; then lions screwed things up and ran another herd off as we closed to within striking distance. It was that kind of a day.

Late in the afternoon we found one last band of the beasts moving en masse toward the watery security of the swamp, the telltale egrets and tick birds keeping track of the Mbogos' wanderings as the cows led the good-sized herd away.

"If we go like hell, we may be able to cut them off before they get to the water, but if they reach the deep stuff, they're gone for today. I've been here before, and it's really ugly in there," Schalk said, watching the herd move like wraiths in the heat-distorted, shimmering distance through his binoculars from the back of the truck.

Grabbing the rifles along with the other necessary accoutrements required for a buffalo stalk, Barraca, our experienced Masai tracker, set a brisk pace to cut off the herd. A deep channel of swamp water forced us to negotiate a detour around it. That messed up our timing, so that when we climbed to the top of a big bush-capped termite mound to get a better look at our prey, all we could see were the rear ends of the slowpokes of the herd as they meandered into the 10-foot tall reed grass.

"Shucks," or perhaps, "Doggonit," or something along those lines sputtered in Afrikaans from Schalk's lips while we watched the reeds swaying back and forth as the herd pushed in deeper. To all of our delight though, 10 minutes later as we sat glassing and hoping, some of the rear guard of the buff herd got the great idea that they still needed an evening snack before they settled into the swamp for the night and began feeding back in the open plains below the termite mound.

None of the buff that emerged had any respectable headgear, unfortunately, at least not respectable enough to make the long journey back to Seattle, so we continued to glass as the majority of the herd continued to meander about in the tall stuff. Every once in a while, sparse sections of the grass would reveal a couple of bulls that might be worth a better look if we could ever get them to cooperate and venture back into the open.

The herd of buffalo heading for the long grass

The mound we were perched on was only 75 to 150 yards from the beasts so we had an up close view of the unsuspecting animals. Schalk and the trackers whispered back and forth to one another in Swahili. Although I could only pick up bits and pieces of the discourse, I could comprehend enough to tell by the tone of their voices that Barraca and Ngatai, our other great tracker, didn't like whatever Schalk was cooking up for them. A few more minutes of jabbering, then the two trackers reluctantly descended the hill behind us and worked their way off to our left.

"What's up, Schalk?" Mack whispered.

"I told them to circle around through the swamp and let the buffalo get their wind. That should make them come back out this way and pass by us."

I looked at Mack to make sure I had heard Schalk correctly and said, "What if the buffalo don't do as planned? It's pretty thick in there, and Barraca won't know how close he is to the bulls until he's too close."

Schalk stared over at the sun as it kissed the horizon and quipped, "Yeah, that's exactly what Barraca said."

As we watched from the safety of our perch, the two Masai moved quickly along the edge of the tall grass, testing the wind while looking for an opening to wade through. When they were a good 100 yards in front of the herd, Schalk got their attention with a low whistle, pointing toward the swamp implying, *"Git yur ass in there, boys!"*

Barraca made a sign back that would not be considered by most to be a friendly gesture before pushing through the sharp reeds toward where they could begin to approach the buff.

As soon as the Masai were directly upwind, the whole herd became agitated, huffing and raising their wet black noses in the air before beginning a mass retreat toward the short grass open ground in front of us. More than half of the huge herd was where we could see them clearly again, but we still could not see a shooter among them.

Then the buffalo, still milling about in the tall swamp grass, decided they were not going out in the open after all and began to push back into the thick stuff, straight at our unsuspecting trackers. Schalk let out a loud two-fingered whistle, a prearranged signal to the guys to say, *"Watch out! The buff are coming back."*

Ngatai started yelling like a crazed cattle driver at the unseen herd, turning them once more toward the open plain, but not for long...Several of the matriarchal cows in the herd simply did not like going along with our plan at all, turning away from the escaping others, heading straight back at the black lads in the thick stuff.

Barraca and Ngatai had made their way to where the buff had trampled down a wide swath through the swamp so they could now see well as the cows pushed straight for them. When the boys realized what was up, they began to thrash the reeds and yell to try once more to turn the black beasts around. From the abrupt change in their demeanor, it seemed that once the cows saw the black men, they decided they were not afraid of them at all, pushing en masse, grunting, thrashing their massive heads back and forth and generally making it known that they were not happy.

Barraca and Ngatai high-stepped it behind some thick stuff to get out of sight which temporarily confused the herd. They whipped their tails back and forth, snorting in great wafts of human scent, becoming more and more enraged as their confidence grew.

Barraca had enough of this and frustratingly began yelling at us to *"Bwana, piga, piga moja!"* (Kill, kill one!)

The yelling accomplished the desired effect and sent the buffalo back toward the opening once again, and when Ngatai saw that the retreat had begun, he ran back out into the opening, charging after the retreating bunch, waving his arms, shouting at the top of his lungs.

"It never fails. When you want them to run when they smell you, they won't," our PH lamented.

"Whoa, check out the bull on the far side of the herd," Mack said. "There's two decent ones in there, see them?"

This was the first glimpse we had of anything worthwhile, so hoping they would continue on the path they were lumbering along on, we scrambled off the termite mound, wading through knee-deep water, directly at where we hoped they would emerge from the high grass.

While lots of animals came out close to us, the good bulls remained on the far side of the herd, blocked from any possibility of a shot by a multitude of black buff bodies.

We pushed forward into the now totally confused milling herd, the leading cows having no clue which way to go. I had my .577 Nitro ready while Mack carried his famed .375 H&H Kenai

Ngatai and Barraca

Crippler at attention, searching for a shot. It was my turn to have first shot this evening, Mack having killed another dandy the night before. So when we saw that the bulls were going to be beyond my comfort zone for shooting a double rifle with iron sights, we swapped weapons.

The herd began parting in front of us as if Moses were leading the way until Schalk slyly crouched, took a couple of quick steps

Sneaking up on the herd after the boys had pushed them back out

forward, then set up the shooting sticks in front of me, quietly saying, "He's the one behind the cow with the white spot on her back. Get ready; he may clear any minute now."

Sho 'nuff, as if on cue, the cow with the white tattoo stepped to her right, giving a clear path to the bull. I squeezed one off, feeling like it was a good shot. The blast had the expected effect of sending the herd in a swarming frenzy, milling around in a circle before splitting in two, half heading for open ground, the rest back toward the trackers. Barraca was screaming as loud as he could, trying to turn them before giving up and running on Ngatai's heels into the safety of the thick stuff.

Luckily for all concerned, the wounded bull followed the herd out into the open, having a hard time keeping up with the rest. As we ran after them hoping for more shots at the staggered bull, he broke free of the bunch and gave me another opening, so I shot at him again, offhand this time, hitting him squarely on his departing right hip. As I reloaded on the run, the bull came to a stop, turning in circles to see where the pain was coming from, ready to take on all comers like a boxer up against the ropes in the corner of the ring in round 12. The rest of the herd held up their flight, waiting for the old patriarch to catch up. The bull was now pacing back and forth, 70 yards behind them, mad as hell.

As we jogged closer to the danger, trying to close the gap before the bull took off with the herd, I once again swapped rifles with Mack, feeling the sense of security swell in my hands at the weight of the Alex Henry canon.

The bull was hurt bad, blood oozing from the bullet holes, a froth of pink painted around his lips as he suddenly spun on his heels to face us at 30 short yards. I took two more steps forward, raising the British double to my shoulder, now standing clear of my compadres.

Realizing the bull had had enough of our fun and games as he raised his great head and began to charge, I put the first bullet below his chin into the center of his chest and as he staggered at the shock of 650 grains of lead raking the length of his worn-out body, I let the second barrel bark, hitting him in the spine over the top of his boss when he dropped his head exposing the sweet spot. That dropped him in his tracks, leaving us all standing staring at the magnificent creature, with that pang of guilt that always accompanies killing one of God's creatures, mixed with the euphoria of the culmination of a true hunt.

While not the biggest bull we had ever killed, he was an old boy, scarred from innumerable battles with lions and rivals, making him a hell of a fine trophy.

A hard-won old dagga boy

Florida Gator

"ALAIN, YOU BETTER GET down here as soon as you can. We got a big ol' gator causin' all kinds of trouble for a rancher down here, and I don't know how long he'll hang around. When could you be here?"

Unbelievably, I was actually at home when the call came from Lee at Outwest Farms in Okeechobee, Florida. Typically, I would be in another country on another adventure when a call like this came through and would have missed the opportunity. Lee's policy is to call his clients when he has located gators that need to be removed after they get into trouble with farmers, ranchers, or when a neighborhood starts loosing Daisy, Duke, or Fluffy to one of the local saurian dinosaurs.

"Let me check flights, but if I can get a flight tomorrow I'll be there."

"Perfect. Call me back as soon as you know what's happening. Now, you did say you wanted a big one, right?"

"Yeah," I replied, remembering that he had a pay-by-the-length policy after you kill one. I swear I heard a smile over the phone as he said,

"Good. Well, we'll see you soon, then. I've got everything you need so don't bring any guns or anything, just your clothes."

Checking with the airlines as soon as I hung up the phone, I found a direct nonstop flight from Seattle to Orlando available the

117

next morning and was on it at eight. Renting a car upon arrival, I showed up around six in the evening at the thriving metropolis of Okeechobee and checked into the hotel. Then I called Lee to let him know I'd arrived. He said, "Hey, I've got a problem that has come up, but the guy who does most of my hunts with me, Casey Lumpkin, will pick you up in half an hour. Can you be ready?"

"Sure," I replied. "What do I need to wear, hip waders, rain gear, knee-high rubber boots? We going to get wet?"

"Naw, just some hiking boots or tennis shoes will be fine."

"Am I going in a boat, or an air boat, or something like that out in the swamp?"

"No, no, no. This one is in a cattle pond at a rancher's place. Regular boots are OK."

I have to admit I had no idea what he was talking about since everything I had seen on his Web site about his hunting operation involved boats and spotlights and splashing-around-in-the-swamp-at-night kind of hunting. So being the I-don't-trust-what-anyone-says kind of guy that I am, I loaded my daypack with rain gear, a change of clothes, and put on my rubber knee-high boots, just in case. If there is one thing I learned from the legendary high-tech redneck Mack Padgett through the years, it's "Don't leave home without your rain gear."

Casey arrived at the hotel in his four-door/four-wheel drive pickup truck not long after I was ready and the adventure began. A nice young guy full of piss and vinegar who loves to hunt and fish in some of the best outdoors America has to offer, we got to know each other as we headed to our destination an hour away.

Turning off the main road, we drove through a rancher's front yard. Casey honked his horn as we passed to let the rancher, who stood watching us from his front-room window as we drove by, know it was us. He waved before turning back to his television. Ten minutes of weaving through the rancher's sparse pasture brought us to a locked gate where my guide said, "All right, let's get out here. We have to walk about ten minutes, but we need to be quiet as we approach the water."

"Are we getting in a boat or what's the plan? Where's the rifle?"

Young Mister Lumpkin chuckled and replied, "No, we aren't using a boat. This gator is in a cattle pond and has been eating this guy's cows when they come to water. There's two of 'em in there. The smaller one is probably his girlfriend, and we don't want to shoot her by mistake."

"Ah, OK," I dumbfoundedly replied, having no idea how all this was going to work. "Where's the rifle?"

"We can't use a rifle at night on these government-controlled hunts, so we are going to use a bow."

At some point, enough is enough, and I had to inform my young skipjack of a guide that, "I have some bad news for you. I don't know which end of the string to pull on a bow, so this could be tough going, amigo."

"No, no, not that kind of bow. I have a crossbow with a scope. You shoot it just like a rifle. It's sweet and right on the money, trust me," he whispered in the glow of the truck's dome light.

Uncasing the deadly contraption from the hard case he carried it in to protect it from the beating it would otherwise take in the back of the truck, he handed it to me along with a couple of extra arrows he called bolts. The contraption held a spool on the killing end of it, wrapped with a high-tensile strength fishing line that was fixed to an arrow with an expandable head designed to catch and hold fish—big fish. The thin strand didn't look strong enough to real some big-ass gator back in, but by this point I had quit asking stupid questions, deciding to go with the flow and see what would happen. Beholding the medieval weapon in my hands, all I could think was, *There is going to be some kind of whacky excitement tonight, Al Smith!*

Off we trudged into the pitch-black darkness, not using our headlamps for fear of scaring the gator. After a few minutes, Casey turned and whispered in my ear, "The wind is perfect. Stay right behind me and when we get to the pond, I'll make sure it's the right one, flip on my flashlight, and you shoot him in the ear hole. Wait for a broadside shot, OK? We have to go slow so he doesn't get scared and go under water."

Nodding my head at the obvious, we continued on at a pace that was faster than I would have taken, as there was no sneaking whatsoever involved in the process at all. We walked up to the pond. There was the gator. My guide pointed at him, and the beast submerged.

"Kaka," or something to that effect came from my mouth. "How long will he stay down for now?"

"Who knows? Usually no more than 15 minutes or so. Go out on the little jetty there and get yourself into a good shooting position and be ready for when he comes back up."

I did as told, surveying my field of fire, realizing that the pond was big enough that if the reptile came up on the far side I would have to move to get close enough for a shot, but from where I was, I could shoot at him if he came up anywhere else on the surface.

I had not been waiting for 5 minutes when 20 yards directly in front of me, the monstrous head of an alligator morphed on the surface, barely making a ripple in the water as it emerged, checking out its lair. My guide, sitting right behind me, whispered, without even using his binos or a flashlight, "That's him. When I flip on the light, shoot him, OK?"

Through the cheap scope I could see perfectly without the light and found the honey hole behind his eye near the ear hole. The angle was perfectly broadside so as soon as the light came on, I squeezed the trigger of the crossbow, sending the deadly shaft of steel into the saurian's cranium. I was shocked to see the gator's lack of reaction when the arrow struck him perfectly. A nerve-induced shiver ran from his head to his tail, a stiff-legged shudder, and then the body slowly rose to the surface.

"Great shot! Nice one. You got him," shouted my guide who jumped up and began gently pulling the string attached to the arrow toward us, the floating and presumably dead dinosaur bobbing along on the surface, ready to be converted into a new purse or pair of Jimmy Choo shoes.

When the gator was within 10 yards of the shore, he got hung up on the gently sloping sandy bottom. Casey dug into his pack and out came a stout rope with a nasty-looking grappling hook attached to one end. Like a pirate boarding a ship full of booty, he tossed the rope across the gator's back, pulled gently until the hook was near the scaly side of the beast, then yanked back for all he was worth, burying the hook in the alligator's side just behind the shoulder. That's when we found out our reptilian prize was not dead...

All hell broke loose as the gator started doing that rolling spin that crocs and gators are so well known for, the pond frothing a filthy brown as the bottom was churned up to the surface. Both of us held tightly to the rope while the pissed off alligator fought for all he was worth. It was at this point that we both got our first real look at the whole length and girth of the monster. Casey whistled, "Damn, look at the size of this thing."

The rope was now getting nice and tangled around the midsection of the body and as the thrashing subsided, it gave us a chance to slowly ease the roped up gator toward shore.

"How are we going to kill this thing?" I asked, holding on with all my strength.

"Dang it, I forgot the bang stick. You hold him where he is, and I'll run back to the truck and get it," was the answer I received.

I wanted to say, "I have a better idea, bubba. How about you hold him and I'll go get the stick?" but I didn't as my guide disappeared into the dark leaving me alone with my headlamp shining on the cold deadly eyes of the gator, staring at me, ready to punish me for what I'd done to him. As I waited, I began to silently estimate this monster's size and figured he had to be at least 12 feet long, maybe longer, and who knew his weight.

The gator laid calmly on the surface, his head facing directly at me, the giant tail giving an occasional menacing sweep to keep itself level while its eyes kept locked on mine. I stayed alert, assuming the gator could cover the short distance between us in a nanosecond if he so chose. Killing time as I waited, I made a mental plan on how I was going to leap to the side, his snapping jaws just missing my torso, like a matador with a charging bull, if he came for me...riiiiggghht...My imagination at this juncture was obviously getting the best of me, and I was sober!

Hearing Mrs. Lumpkin's brightest running back to the pond settled my nerves instantly. My partner proceeded to load the ammo into the homemade bang stick. The idea with these gizmos that have a 4½ foot long shaft is that you break open the hinged end of it, stick a .45 caliber round in, snap it closed, and it's ready to go. Then when hard pressure is applied to the tip, the charge goes off, sending the bullet into the intended victim's gray matter.

"OK, here's what we are going to do. I'm going to pull on the rope and get this gator's head up on the shoreline, and you are going to hit him between the eyes with this here bang stick, got it?"

"Sure."

"OK, here we go. Git ready."

As he tugged on the rope, the reptilian behemoth began floating toward us. I soon figured out that because of the size and length of the head, I was going to have to lean way out over the gator's nose or get in the water next to it to be able to place the cartridge where it needed to go. As I stepped into the water, Casey shouted, "Don't go in the water. This gator'll git yur ass."

Backpedaling just as the gator made a lunge for me, I tried my best leaping out of the way, while stabbing at his head with the bang stick, missing 6 inches to the right in my haste. The bang from the .45 going off in his head really gave the reptile a new sense of pissedoffedness, sending him back to thrashing around wildly 4 feet offshore.

"You missed the brain. Load up and try it again, damn it," he shouted again while he did his best to hold on.

I quickly reloaded, wishing the bang stick had a 20 foot long shaft on it as I prepared for the next onslaught. The rope tightened, the gator slid smoothly forward, and just as I went in for the kill, he opened his mouth giving me a close look at a nasty row of his pearly whites. I leapt up and came down like some sort of spastic Spaniard putting the sword into a charging bull at the Madrid ring,

Crossbow bolt in the right spot

but missed the brain once again in my ungainly effort. The shot did rattle the gator this time, however, slowing his thrashing to a more manageable pace as I reloaded once more.

I could tell my junior guide was beginning to wonder what he had got himself into as he held on for dear life, jumping out of the way as the alligator would surge forward, intent on getting a bite out of the knuckleheads that ruined his holiday in the cattle pond.

"All right, let's try this again. Slide him up here one more time," I yelled over the racket of the gator's thrashings.

Casey yanked hard and up slid the reptile. I juked to the right, then high-stepped to the left, concentrating the whole time on the spot just behind the center of his eyes, and plunged the bang stick home. At the report of the shell, the pond became deathly still. Other than a couple of nerve-induced twitches of the tail, the gator finally appeared to be dead.

"Way to go, man, way to go," whooped Casey. "I'm going to go get the truck. I'll be right back."

I sat on the bank to catch my breath and admire my trophy, although I couldn't see any part of the body behind the midsection as it was submerged below the muddy surface. When the truck returned, I grabbed the rope that was wound around the beast and tied it to the trailer hitch. I gave directions while Casey eased the pickup forward, tightening the rope. The big rear tires began to spin in the soft soil around the pond due to the tremendous weight of the reptile until he put it in four-wheel drive.

The monster slowly slid out of the pond as the truck struggled in low gear. One foot after another, it began emerging from the water. What an animal! I had never even seen a picture of one this size; never even realized they got this big. Disconnecting the rope and turning the truck around so we could use the headlights on the alligator, we began to unravel the rope tangled about his carcass— until the tail moved and the head twitched a foot to the left. Both of us jumped back as if we had been electrocuted.

Casey prepping the gator...

Casey hesitantly mumbled, "Maybe we should duct tape his jaws shut."

"Yeah, that sounds like a good idea," I nervously laughed, standing well outside the gator's grasp. Sitting on the beast's head, we eased the roll of tape around his nose until after several wraps of the silver tape our confidence returned enough to relax and enjoy the moment and admire our prize.

We had to run back to the farmhouse and ask if we could borrow the farmer's tractor with a front end loader on it so we could load the monster into the back of the truck. The owner of the land was more than happy to accommodate us, considering how many calves the gator had eaten in the past few weeks.

It turned out the gator really was a monster when it was officially measured the next day. He weighed in at 938 pounds and was 13 feet 4 inches in length when measured from the tip of his nose to the point of his tail. What a trophy!

Now that's a gator

Markhor Madness

O NE OF THE GREAT conservation success stories in the past 100 years has been the Markhor of Pakistan. These spiral-horned Capras inhabiting the cliffs and mountains of some of the most remote places on earth have made a comeback to the point where we hunter/conservationists can now pursue them, *if we dare*, on their home turf.

There are three species of true Markhor in Pakistan; the Astor from the Chitral area, the Suleiman from the Torghar Mountains in the northeast section of Balochistan, and the Kashmir of the Khosistan area in the northwest part of the country. The Chiltan wild goat is also found in western Pakistan; however, it is not a pure Markhor. It is considered by most biologists to be a mutt, a cross between Markhor and domestic goats at some point in its family lineage, which is a regular occurrence wherever their ranges overlap.

The only other huntable population of Markhors is found in Uzbekistan, these being the Bukharin subspecies. However, the Uzbeks rarely hand out one of the coveted permits and have not done so in several years now.

The Suleiman Markhor (*Capra falconeri jerdoni*) is considered to be of the straight-horned variety. How any scientist came up with the term "straight horned" to describe the Suleiman, which has a tight, corkscrew twist to their horns, unlike their cousin the

Kashmir Markhor whose horns flare out and curl skyward much like the African kudu, is beyond me. It is the equivalent of saying that chopsticks are a member of the spoon family.

Saving the Suleiman Markhor from extinction can be directly credited to the tireless work of the late Nawab Taimur Shah Jogizai, a visionary tribal leader and avid hunter who ruled vast tracks of the Torghar region. After seeing firsthand the decimation of the wildlife by local as well as refugee poachers from neighboring Afghanistan, each one of them armed with the ubiquitous Kalashnikov, he initiated the Torghar Conservation Program (TCP) in 1986. According to the first survey he commissioned that year, he discovered that the Markhor were hovering at a dismal 56 animals and the Afghan urials at less than 100 animals.

His first step after creating TCP was to ban all hunting/poaching of Markhor and urial under his jurisdiction. His next act was to hire the best poachers from the region, turning them into armed patrols and scouts to protect the animals as well as educate the subsistence-level living tribesman and nomads that historically crossed through his area with their goats about saving the wildlife. Severely punishing a few of the early poachers to make examples of them for the rest of the people to see, the Nawab soon had everyone's attention as to what was going on with the wildlife in the area and that he was serious about saving them.

From the beginning, the Nawab and his people had a plan that if they could recover the animal populations to a sustainable use level, they would be able to raise money selling hunting permits to foreigners, thereby bringing much-needed cash into the area and making the project viable for all community members. The project was funded from day 1 only by the Nawab and private donations. No government intervention was requested or accepted, which made the project run smoothly and without politics involved.

Sardar Naseer Tareen also joined the project not long after its inception using his education, filmmaking skills, and contacts with government agencies to move the project through the hoops necessary to take it to the next level. Through Mr. Tareen's contacts, he was able to get several well-known scientists on board and U.S. Fish and Wildlife involved in the project. The agency devoted some manpower and science to the project, adding creditability with the expressed *written* goal that in the end, sustainable use through hunting a few of the excess older males would be the main ingredient to keeping the Markhor recovery a reality.

The obvious key to sustainable use is that the money raised from issuing a paltry few permits each year provides income to the local people, who, then, voluntarily, keep their domestic sheep and goats out of certain parts of the mountains, creating a better habitat for the Markhor, while having ceased all poaching of the animals for meat.

The sad truth of the project has been that every player in the process of saving the Markhor has done his job well and kept his word—except the United States Fish and Wildlife Service.

Numbers of the animals have increased now to the point where CITES (Convention on International Trade in Endangered Species), a very conservative guardian of wildlife resources worldwide and the organization that most countries of the world abide by, honoring its rules and permit process, has issued four permits per year for the export of the hunted trophies of this endangered species.

U.S. F&W, however, has in its infinite wisdom, rejected the findings and is not honoring the valid CITES permits, arbitrarily deciding that Americans (who make up 90 percent of worldwide big game hunters willing to spend the astronomical fees required to hunt a Markhor) *cannot* bring their hard-won trophies home to the good ol' U.S. of A. This has made selling the few available permits very difficult for the tribal area and hurts the project's over-all sustainability.

The TCP is today well managed under the watchful eyes of the current Nawab Mahoob Joganzi living in the mountains and Mr. Tareen and Paind Khan based out of Quetta, a bumpy 6 hours by Jeep from the mountain-hunting area.

I decided the hell with it and regardless of whether I could or could not bring home a Suleiman Markhor, I wanted to hunt them while at the same time helping the conservation program in Pakistan. So in February of 2011, I finally made the long journey to a small village northwest of Quetta, a known hotbed for al-Qaeda types, to hunt one of the great animals on this terra firma we call planet Earth.

The trip was organized by the guru of Asian hunting, Kaan Karakaiya, and his company, Shikar Safaris, in conjunction with

Street vendor in Quetta

their Pakistani partner Farhod Maqpoon. Along on the trip from Shikar's Turkish office were Serkan Mert, and from Pakistan, Ejaz Ali, the man who spends countless hours in the mountains prescouting top trophies for incoming hunters. My compadre on the trip who was there to collect one of the Afghan urials that inhabit the lower reaches of the steep mountains was Dennis Anderson, past president of Safari Club International and still today a tireless worker for conservation through the Safari Club Foundation, some pretty heady company for me, an immigrant refugee from Prince Albert, Saskatchewan.

Arriving at the brick and mud one-story building built in the proverbial "middle of nowhere," complete with a bedroom and sit-down toilet, however, sans shower en suite, I looked at my watch. It was eight in the evening local time. I began running through the hours involved since I had left my home in Seattle.

"Dennis, my friend, I make it out to be somewhere around 59 hours of travel, with only 6 hours in a bed, since I left home. That sound about right to you?"

Pouring a wee dram of rum into a glass for each of us, topped off with a couple ounces of local orange juice, Dennis laughed and said, "I think you're about right and a couple of these babies and a full night's sleep is going to feel real good, buddy."

Did it ever...

Waking before dawn and organizing my kit to make sure I was prepared for the day's adventure, we ate a quick breakfast, swilled down some instant coffee, then gathered outside with the local hunting guides to devise a plan of attack. Mingling awkwardly with the dozen Mujahideen-garbed gents, I must admit to feeling rather wimpy in this crowd, what with my clean shaven face and recently coiffed hair. All the macho-type locals wore dirty turban-type head-gear wrapped loosely around unruly hair and beards dancing in the cold morning breeze.

Suleiman game scout

There really is something terrifically manly about never shaving, wearing a turban, loose-fitting pajamas, and having an AK 47 slung casually over your shoulder as an accoutrement to complete "the look." I don't suppose it would be a good idea to attempt this fashion statement in Manhattan on a Friday night, but all in all, you gotta think it's a pretty cool image.

Dennis and some of the crew, it had been decided, were taking one of the Land Cruisers to an area where several large urial rams had been spotted recently, while my crew of 20 people, including cameramen, local guides, the head honcho of the area, Paind Kahn, and my amigos from the hunting companies, would begin walking right from camp into the steep surrounding mountains.

An explanation is in order at this point to explain what these mountains are like in the Torghar region. Rising steeply up from the rocky barren rolling plains below, this dry, sandy moonscape holds very little wildlife of any kind other than the wild sheep and Markhor. How the domestic sheep and goats scratch out a living I have no idea since there is very little vegetation in the surrounding plains available to eat.

Torghar Mountains

The people herding livestock live a subsistent-based, poverty-racked life, their housing being fashioned from large sheep wool blankets used as tents and rag-covered pits built partially underground to help fight off the severe cold in the winter and the excruciating heat of the summers. Firewood is in short supply after centuries of civilization clawing away at the environment, and the few trees I did stumble across were definitely nervous...

Some of the more well-to-do people live in rustic mud-brick-fashioned one-room shacks, but still below poverty level living conditions by any measure.

Off my gang and I went, walking one behind the other, working our way along a dry creek bottom for a mile or so before beginning to climb up the steep slopes, grasping for handholds in many places when the going got too tough for mere mortal bipeds. We stopped frequently to rest under the cloud-covered gray sky, aching to let its rain-filled load dump on us at this typically dry time of year.

The goatherds' trail leading south along the Afghan border we trekked was easy to follow, the local guides keeping a brisk pace with an obvious unrevealed destination in mind. I have found after all these years of following guides around in ridiculous corners of the world that it's usually best to not ask too many questions about what's going on or where are we going and just follow the leader. Since it's his job to get you to the animal you are after, my job to kill it, I follow as instructed, but I was still somewhat puzzled that we rarely stopped to glass or "hunt" as we trudged along, quickly following the spine of the mountain range, one determined step after another.

After a good 3 hours of hiking, we eventually came to a huge outcropping, with a view of several miles in almost any direction, and sat down to use the binos for their intended purpose while snacking on some Jack Link's beef jerky I had brought along for just such an occasion. I have to admit to being greedy with the jerky, only slipping the odd piece out of my pocket and slyly into

Local guides glassing

my mouth when not too many of my entourage would be looking in my direction. After all, a couple packs of jerky smuggled all the way over from America do not go far if you start sharing with the 20-odd locals hanging out with you, right?

A slight drizzle began falling from the blackening clouds as we searched the nooks and crannies for the monster Markhor the guys kept saying hung out in this area. We were certainly seeing plenty of females and youngsters from where we sat. In any direction you could easily find bands of five to 20 of the wild goats, browsing on the sheer slopes, dancing from rocky ledges to vertical cliffs. There was a mixture of young males mixed in with the family groups, but I was somewhat surprised at how few big billies we were spotting considering the total number of Markhor we could see.

Paind was the first one to get excited when he finally found three mature males, nonchalantly chewing their cud, sheltered out of the wind on a fractured cliff face a long, long ways away from us. Putting the Swarovski 60 power spotting scope on the animals, we could easily see that all of them were shooters, with one being an outstanding-looking specimen.

This group was "too far away to get to today," said Paind, "but we can always get them tomorrow." A couple of the guys on my left then began jabbering to each other before they motioned for me to come over where they were sitting and take a look. Not 200 yards away, standing regally below us with his harem of nannies and kids feeding around him, stood a fantastic long-horned representative of the Suleiman species. My heart jumped as I watched in awe the majesty of the grand Markhor standing broadside, surveying his domain. But my heart fell to my stomach when the billy turned, revealing that he only had one fantastic horn, the other side being broken off two inches above the hairline. In discussion with the as-sembled crew, it was confirmed by all that if he had matching horns, this patriarch would definitely be the world record.

After 2 hours of searching, it was decided we should make a move further up the mountain range. The time was slipping by, and we had a long walk back to camp, especially if the black clouds gath-ering above us decided to open up their fury upon us.

As we snuck along, the guys spread out, searching each of the spiny ridges jutting off from the main mountain we were hiking across. Cautiously easing up over a dangerous-looking drop-off, the two guides in front of me abruptly ducked down, looking back at me and making the wild pantomime to *load my rifle and get ready!* I blindly did as instructed, praying it was my turn to see my first trophy Markhor up close and personal.

Ejaz came alongside of me with the video camera, and then, on cue, we both eased ever so slowly over the top of the ridge and quickly found two big Markhor males nibbling at bushes while casu-ally surveying their kingdom below. The head guide lying between us quietly mumbled something to Ejaz, who translated to me.

The rain turned to snow

"He says there is another bigger one behind the huge boulder. Can you see it? I can't see from where I am."

I searched through my Swarovski scope set on 12 power until I found what he was talking about. I could just make out the top 6 inches of two corkscrew horns, bobbing above the boulder.

"Yes, I see his horns. Look at the very top edge of the boulder to the right of the last Markhor."

Ejaz found him in the camera lens and began rolling the tape. The guide said, "Wait for the big one; don't shoot the two we can see." No problem, I figured as I settled in for a 185-yard shot if the billy would just step out.

After 3 or 4 minutes of anxiously waiting, the second billy took several steps forward, munching fresh twigs as he passed by a thorny green bush. The Markhor in the lead was beginning to get nervous, staring up at the plateau we were all lying on. I could sense he was going to bolt at any minute when the Markhor in the rear suddenly stopped feeding and looked straight at us as well. I held my sights on the spot where the rear goat had been standing, praying that the big one would step forward a couple paces and give me a chance at him.

As if my pleadings were answered by the Almighty himself, the hidden Markhor stepped forward into the clear wondering what his buddies were staring at. That was all the chance I needed and a millisecond after I squeezed the Bansner .7 mm's trigger, the billy leapt forward at the impact of the bullet striking him just behind the shoulder and sent him crashing to the bottom of the rocky canyon. Cheers went up from the AK 47 crowd with lots of backslapping accompanied by whooping and hollering at our success.

Even though we were only 185 yards away as the crow flies, it still took us 25 minutes to work our way around the steep walls and cliffs until we found a semisafe way to get to the Markhor's final resting place.

The king of the corkscrews

I'm a lucky guy, and I've had the pleasure to have a lot of super animals in my hands over the years, but I have got to say that to hold a Suleiman Markhor's horns in my hands was a great honor and privilege I will not soon forget.

Suleiman Markhor

Convergence

SOMETIMES THINGS HAPPEN FOR no rhyme or reason. They just happen...

You get up in the morning, you plan out your day, thinking everything will go as planned since you are prepared, practiced, and practical.

Unfortunately for you, depending on what fate's fickle fingers deal you this fine morning, the universe's unbending laws require that somewhere out there in the vast beyond, someone or something is preparing for their day as well, prepared, practiced, and practical.

Now, for who knows why, it has been deemed by Nature's twisted logic that you and that someone or something's paths are going to cross at an exact, defined moment this fine day. It could be good, or it could be bad; you have no say in it. It's just the way it is.

It's called convergence.

Rising at five fifteen in the morning, just like every other morning, the cool darkness that engulfed our Western Tanzania hunting camp felt good on my Northwestern U.S.A. sunburned skin.

"Today," I tell myself, "I am putting on lotion to quell the near-equatorial golden orb's power."

But I'll forget to again in the rush to get dressed and join the others at the breakfast table, quietly sipping good strong coffee, with their choices for breakfast given to the camp boy in broken Swahili and English.

"Leta chai and ningependa machungwa eh mkate."

Abdul, in his starched white linen waiter's shirt, understands the American accented order of tea, oranges, and toast, and then hustles the 30 yards to the smoky kitchen to help prepare the bwana's order to perfection, or at least as best as can be done 800 miles from anywhere. The dark tea I'm sipping washes the pills down my unshaven throat, hopefully dulling the pain from last night's celebratory cocktails in liquid tribute to an outstanding sable antelope shot well by the other appreciative hunter in camp.

I rub at my temples, begging for the pounding to go away, waiting for the rush from the caffeine and the pharmaceuticals to get the new day off on the right foot.

"So, my lily-livered friends, what say we go out and have ourselves a good old-fashioned buffalo hunt in the swamp today? The big herd should still be on the dry island along the river to the north of here unless something spooked them. Shall we give them a try?" asked my PH, looking as bad as I feel this humid morning.

"I'm in," I say, not giving it a second thought.

"Me too," chimes in my hunting buddy.

After all, Cape buffalo hunting, to any adrenaline junky, is so much fun, it's hard to believe that it's legal.

~2~

The 4-year-old male lion listened as dawn's eerie light began to turn the blackness to a cool slate gray. He waited for the morning grunting call of one of the older males hunting somewhere in the distance or the growl of a female gathering her pride to begin another hunt while the temperature still made sense, but he heard nothing.

Just as it had been now for weeks, each day it seemed there were fewer responses to his chest-heaving grunts signaling he, as a young male not settled into his own pride yet, was here in the area, ready to take over someone's pride. Usually an immediate warning response came from one of the older males letting him know he was going to get his ass kicked bad if he came any nearer to the big lion's girlfriends and kittens.

The young lion, having learned the hard way, still nursing a torn ear that would leave a ragged scar for the rest of his days, hovered in the safe zone around the pride he could smell in the still morning air, picking through the scraps left over from the females' buffalo kill earlier in the week.

Lately though, the lion prides had found a much-easier target than buffalo: cattle. The cattle, illegally brought into the lush government hunting concession by Rwanda-based former rebels who bribed local officials, chiefs, and game wardens to turn a blind eye to the intrusions, ate freely of the bountiful waist-high grass growing there, driving the other wildlife into less-than-lush sectors of the park.

The cattle herders, carrying their ubiquitous AK 47s left over from the war, also helped themselves to any free *ngama* they might stumble upon, like say a roan antelope, perhaps one of the beautiful black sable antelope, or better yet, one of Kigosi's bull elephants carrying 70 pounds of ivory to a side, that not only supplied a couple tons of meat to feed the herd boys, but brought the boss $2,000 or more on the black market for the ivory tusks. Elephants, they had found, tend to be much more profitable than cattle.

Unfortunately, as soon as the lions developed a taste for the easy-to-catch hay burners, the herders quickly responded ruthlessly. Since lions are born with a propensity to return to their kills after satiating themselves with the first course, then sleeping off the gorge for 12 or more hours, it is easy for the cattlemen to find their dead heifers, run the lions off with shouting and shooting, then poison the remaining carcass with a mixture of arsenic and antifreeze, knowing the lions will return within a day and die an excruciatingly painful death soon after they finish what remains of the poisoned beef.

The really devilish thing about poisoning is that the carcass not only kills marauding lions, but eagles, storks, vultures, jackals, hyena, and any other creature that scavenges a meal from the tainted cow. This is done all in the name of illegal cattle in areas set aside by the government for protecting wildlife and bringing in hunters who pay a small fortune for the right to take a small percentage of the animals. The funds are then used by the game department, whose most intended purpose is to protect the area; however, graft and corruption, not only as it relates to wildlife, but as a way of doing

Lion sneaking up on an easy meal

daily business on the Dark Continent, will keep Africa mired in the third world forever...

The young male let out a baritone-pitched grunting roar into the chilly fog rising around him at the dry edge of the swamp,

"Grrruuuunnnnnnf, huhhhhhhh, erhuhhhnf, erhuuunf!"

An older female, whose reply he did not recognize, responded with a quieter, "Arghghghghhhh, rugggf, hrrrufff."

Emboldened by the response and hearing no threatening male, he carefully trotted toward the sound, watchful in the dawn fog that there wasn't a big male hanging in ambush with the female. Another lioness let out a couple of softer grunts before he heard some cubs wrestling and squawking at each other.

Seeing the family group through the mist lounging under an ancient acacia tree, looking side to side for a dominant male but seeing none, he strode bravely up to the old female, brushing housecatlike past her, running their whiskers past each other's bodies, sensing a welcoming exchange. The lioness needed a male. Her pride's males had all been poisoned by the tainted cattle so she had intuitively held the rest of the pride back after the initial deaths of the more aggressive males after smelling something strange in the meat of the tame cows the others had killed. It was time to switch their diet back to more tradition fare, Cape buffalo.

With only five full-grown females, two three-year-old males, and a bevy of new kittens, she needed this new male in their pride to help them kill the black beasts of prey as well as breed. The pride needed to kill today. It had been several days without fresh meat while they waited for the rest of the pride to return to the kittens, but they never did.

The old lioness walked away from the others, nose up and into the wind, tasting the breeze. She knew from spending her entire life in Kigosi that the buffalo would be on the dry ground at the edge of the swamp today and that they would run into the thickest wet part

I'm hungry

of the swamp when they were pushed by the pride. There it would be easy to pull down an old or injured buff or perhaps a calf buffalo once it was separated from its mother.

Today the pride would eat.

~3~

The bumpy drive in the Land Cruiser through the gray pillarlike termite mounds seemed quicker if not dustier than past days. The three of us white men stood silently in the back, my partner and I zipped our leather vests to the neck against the dawn chill, the professional hunter bundled in his down coat as if the temperature were below freezing, not the true 75 degrees Fahrenheit it actually was. The Masai trackers behind us wore wool knee-length trench coats, stocking caps pulled tight over their droopy pierced ears, while their yellow-hued malarial eyes scanned the nearing swamp for any telltale signs of today's quarry: Mbogo.

The Cape buffalo in the Kigosi hunting concession have been hammered hard by a deadly concoction of losing precious acres of fodder to the illegal domestic cattle herds, mixed with constant pressure from hunters and poachers when the huge herds congregate in their last bastion of hope, the inner swamp.

The "legal" overhunting has resulted from the concession holder, a politically well-connected Arab businessman from Dar es Salam selling more licenses for animals than his allotted government quota by slipping the crooked game department in the city a few extra Tanzanian shillings as they complete the necessary paperwork for *added quota*. Immediate greed overrides sensible management as he rakes in big bucks from the unsuspecting American hunters who dole out a small fortune after being sold a bill of goods that they will be hunting in an "exclusive area" where no one else will be allowed to hunt. The truth of the matter is the opposite as we found out, stumbling into two other hunting parties during the first 10 days of our grand safari, who were chasing the same herd of buffalo we were.

Our trusted PH, making the best of a bad situation he had no control of until he could return to Dar and ream out the Arab, knew the best way to get away from the crowd is to walk to where no normal, sane hunters will, or are physically able to hike to. We knew after meeting the other hunters in their vehicle a couple days before that they would not have the stamina to make the long trudge to the inner swamp. Practically speaking, the Tsetse flies and swarms of mosquitoes, never mind the leaches and snakes, would definitely turn them back to the security of their vehicle within an hour after they started.

Our team had done this dance before, fully expecting a day of wet boots, sore legs, and more bites than you can scratch when the muck is washed from your burnt hides at the end of the day. But we still revel in the pain since it is one of the few *real hunts* left to intrepid explorers. Like the other heart-pumper hunts, you have to get off the beaten path to find good adventure. It is not waiting anywhere near the side of the truck, so I was surprised to hear the tracker lean forward and hiss to the professional hunter as he pointed off into the distance to our right, *"Poli poli, Bwana. Mbogo!"*

The truck slowed down as directed and sure as hell, after a gaze through our binoculars, there on the haze-filled horizon are the telltale white cattle egrets and rusty-brown tick birds wafting above barely discernable black backs of buffalo, moving slowly, parting the tall, thick, green swamp reeds.

Everyone began to shed the layers of Cabela's finest that they were wearing against the chill, knowing the last thing we were going to need would be a coat once the sun shows itself fully and the midmorning temperatures soar into the 90s.

Nothing is said as each person gathers his kit for the day. I double-check my decades-old daypack before handing it to our other wily Masai tracker, who shoulders it, grabs the wooden shooting sticks out of the bed of the truck, then stands impatiently, ready to go. I buckle my leather culling belt around my waist, made from the first Tembo I killed many years ago, touching each of the cigar-sized brass .577 NE cartridges, making sure they are snug in their loops just in case there ends up being any running involved in today's activities, which seems to be a common occurrence when we buff hunt the old-fashioned way. Up close...

~4~

The lioness caught the faint scent in the still damp air—*buffalo*—just as she suspected. She turned to check on her diminished pride, content that the cubs were still lounging with a lesser-ranking female who would watch over and protect them from the hyena and jackals that would prey on them, while she led the rest into battle. The young males and the new arrival followed her lead as the other lioness jogged to catch up to her. They all had caught the drifting smell of a good meal, quickening their pace in hopes of catching the buff while they still lounged about on this crisp morning. The little puffs of wind that blew from the swamp came straight to them, a perfect setup if it only held steady.

The cats instinctively fanned out, slowing their pace as the smell of the huge herd of Mbogo grew stronger, each one of the lions focusing their keen eyesight on the tall grass ahead, searching for any telltale black patches of the mighty *Syncerus caffer caffer*. Cautiously, the lions crept one tentative step after another, looking from side to side at each other, checking to see if any others in the pride had caught sight of the beasts just beyond the 4-foot-high reeds.

The old lioness saw her daughter freeze out of the corner of her eye, one front foot held in the air, solid, as if she were carved from stone. The rest of the pride pantomimed the lioness's actions before easing onto their bellies, seeking a vision of black themselves. As the frozen lion felt safe moving, she hunched her shoulders before lowering herself into a creeping position, moving one slow motion step after another until she reached the edge of the tall weeds, perfectly camouflaged in the tawny brown grass. The others followed her strategy until reaching the edge of the open savanna as well.

The ground before them held no cover; it had been mowed like a putting green by the multitude of buffalo that now milled 250 yards in front of them. There was nothing the pride could do now but wait and see what the herd would do as some of the buff rose from their beds to join others who had already begun munching on the recently burned pasture where new shoots had sprung up, green, sweet, and full of protein.

Patience is the lion's ally. The old lioness knew it was better to wait out the buffalo then try a risky charge across the open field. The others waited for her to make a decision, statuesquely frozen in place with only their nervous tails twitching in anticipation behind their hungry bodies.

~5~

I felt good now, closing in on the buffalo. (Although photographs later in the day would reveal I still looked hungover, however, the good news was so did everyone else in the glamour shots.) The wind was changing direction, as it deemed necessary, but overall held in our favor. The cover was thin in the dry stretch we had to sneak across, requiring that we crawl from termite mound to bushy patch, then on to the next mound or grassy tussock ahead. The sheer number of Mbogo in this herd made getting close statistically impossible, but we continued on doing our best to remain invisible to the 500 cold black eyes looking out for danger.

My PH, leading the way, turned back and spoke in Swahili to one of the trackers and the government game scout in our entourage, telling them to wait here as we approached closer. The less people the better as we inched closer to the herd. Seeing no objections from the game scout, but disappointment in the Masais' eyes, we left them there to watch the events unfold from a discreet distance.

Gaining another 50 yards of real estate on the buff, we stopped to catch our breath, the heavy .577 nitro slowing my progress as we inched along on hands and thorn-filled knees. Hunkering behind one of the last small termite mounds that proffered any cover at all, we glassed the herd carefully, looking for one of the huge bulls that Tanzania is famous for.

Then I felt the wind tickle the hair on the back of my neck...

~6~

The lioness's whole body tensed as the entire herd of Mbogo suddenly rose to their feet in a panicked frenzy. Milling around in a large circle, not sure which way to go, finally a matriarchal cow impatiently led the herd downwind, away from the scent of man that had appeared out of nowhere, frightening the 250 or more black beasts into flight, which then ran straight at the waiting cats.

The old pussycat held steady, as did all the others lying in wait in the tawny-colored grass. Every muscle was taut, her sinewy form ready to pounce at the appropriate time. The young male lying 10 yards to her right could hardly contain himself. It had been a week since he had eaten last. There was going to be meat for all if the herd kept coming.

As the buffalo closed to within 30 yards, the lioness knew it was time to make a move or else they might all be trampled. She reacted to the 100-yard wide wave of black beasts bearing down on her by standing and showing herself in full view of the lead buff that quickly tried to slow their progress toward their mortal enemy.

The Cape buffalo behind the leaders couldn't see the lions and tried to push onward away from the scent of man behind them, but the forward flanks of bulls slowed them to a seething mass of black and gray dust whirling about them.

The lions had them totally at their mercy now and charged as a precision trained force out of the waist-high grass, causing even more confusion in the panicked buff leaders who tried to spin away from the trouble. The wind suddenly reversed itself, sending the lions' scent toward the herd, causing even greater panic, splitting the herd into two separate herds, one running left and one hightailing it to the right.

The lions took advantage of the confusion, half of them jumping on a young calf's back that had been separated from his normally protective mother, while the remainder of the pride focused on an old dugga boy who fell behind staggering for one moment too long. One young male jumped on top of the old bull, sinking his fangs into the back of the bull's once-mighty neck, as a lioness held tight to the buff's flank, ripping at his stomach with her back paws, opening up his paunch, intestines pouring out of the split hide onto the filth below him. Another female seeing her chance launched her full weight onto the staggering bull's left hindquarter, tripping the once-mighty warrior who fell onto his side, allowing the remainder of the pride to swarm over him. The bull's time had come.

~7~

A word most often associated with the act of coitus emitted from my sun-dried lips as I watched the herd of buffalo run off moments after I had felt the wind kiss the back of my neck. The same word, spoken in Swahili, Afrikaans, and South Carolinian, hissed in three-part harmony from my companions as we watched the mass of black running away for all they were worth heading to our right. We followed our PH's lead and stood up, tired joints reveling in the relief after kneeling for the past hour.

"The damn morning wind is so unpredictable out here in these swamps," sighed our experienced guide, removing his binoculars from his bloodshot eyes. "Let's head back to the truck and see if we can find another herd."

Dejectedly, heads hung low, our troop walked in a free-form file toward where we had left the other two members of our group huddled in the shade of an elephantine gray-colored termite pinnacle. The Masai with us noticed first that the two Africans waiting for us in the shade were waving their arms frantically trying to get our attention. Looking up to see why they were jumping up and down, crazily pointing back toward where the buffalo had run, we all spun in unison to see a big portion of the herd running straight towards us, 150 yards away and closing.

"What the..." the PH muttered.

"This doesn't look good," quipped my famous pig farmer friend in typical Southern understatement.

Now we're going to get a really good look at them was all that went through my testosterone-filled brain at that moment. I know, I need psychiatric help; I can't help myself.

Our exteriorly calm-looking guide waved his hand behind him, indicating we should crouch down again, I suppose in some wacky attempt to hide in the knee-high grass we were kneeling in. It was too late to run; we would never have made it clear of the impending stampede.

I cracked open my .577 to triple-check that it was loaded before I slipped two 650 grain cigar-sized shells from my belt, placing them between the fingers on my left hand, so that I would be able to reload quickly when the time came.

As I loosened up two more rounds on my belt, expecting the worst, I noted everyone else double-checking their .375s as well. The Masai knelt beside me, holding nothing but his Assegai spear, a confident grin covering his jet-black face from ear to ear as the massive herd bore down on us not 40 yards away now. There was nowhere to run to, and the Mbogo were not slowing down as they came full-on in a 70-yard wide swath.

Our PH looked over his shoulder and said over the thundering din of hundreds of hoofs bearing down on us, "We're going to have to do something quick. I'm not sure if they see us or not. When I stand up, you guys do the same and fan out so we all have a shot in case they don't stop when they see us. Headshots only. We need to kill the leaders to stop the stampede."

My .577 Nitro Express felt like a peashooter as I stood up. *At least if the game scout was with us we'd have an extra machine gun.*

I moved to the left as my partner slipped swiftly to the right, assuming the I'm-going-to-shoot-something-right-now pose. I was cold with fear as the stampeding herd saw us rise up and all hell broke loose.

Two young bulls leading a pack of 20 animals 30 yards to our right slid to a halt when we stood up, swinging their massive hooked horns menacingly at us. A cow crashed into one of the bulls as she tried to stop her run, then another cow bashed into her as the bulls created a dam slowing the rest of the herd. The remainder of the herd to our left panicked upon seeing us and sped up their run forward, with each animal giving us a nasty once-over look on their way by.

Our big problem was still the main body of the herd that continued on toward us, seemingly not noticing we were in their way until a scarred old cow lifted her head above the dust, saw us, bellowed a hoarse grunt, and swerved slightly to our left. The rest of the massive herd comprised of cows, calves, and lots of young bulls streamed by us, not 15 yards away, panic in the whites of their eyes, trying to get away from the danger we represented.

The bulls to our right stepped tentatively forward, noses up. The PH and my friend had them covered as I looked for a shooter, or more likely a charger, on my side of the engulfing herd.

The two bulls began a heads-up charge simultaneously as if they were choreographed, kicking their pace into full speed as my buddy leaned into his rifle. I was sure he was going to dust the one on the right's forehead with 270 grains of Mr. Barnes finest copper when the bulls lost their nerve and veered away to the right at 18 yards, the rest of this herd following in their footsteps. The mass of black bodies kept streaming around us, as if we were an island in the middle of a fast-moving river, the bulk of the herd closing ranks after flowing around the four of us, standing with rifles ready to fire at the first sign of any of them getting too close.

I have to admit, even though scared out of my gourd, I was still sizing up every buffalo that came by my side of the island. *Cow, cow, young bull, decent bull but soft bosses, old bull broken horn, cow,* etcetera, but surprisingly didn't see one shooter in the whole bunch.

As the last of the herd streamed by us, grunting and moaning deeply as if they were so many domestic cows upset in a feedlot, the dust swirled around our crew, voiding most of our view beyond 30 feet. Two last cows gave us a cursory mock charge as if to say, "Thanks for wrecking my morning siesta, white boy," but changed their minds seconds before lead would have filled the air.

I turned to see everyone standing, rifles at rest, filthy dust covering everything but the white teeth shining through the nervous smiles of my amigos.

"Not a good bull in bunch," I managed to say through a throat dryer than the Kalahari.

My buddy shook his head in agreement, but our PH replied as he ran a shaky hand through his long sun-streaked hair, pushing it back off his forehead, "On our side, I saw two really good bulls on the outside edge of the herd. Let's get some water, let the herd settle down for an hour or so, and then we can try and get them."

I sat down on a small termite mound, wiping the sweat and mire from my brow with a bandana, hoping no one noticed my whole body shaking as the reality of what had just happened sunk in, and thought, *Maybe I need a new vice?*

Tiny Titans

I WONDER HOW HOT IT *has to get before you just die from it? I hope it's a quick death 'cause I can't take much more of this...* I thought as I wiped the mosquito-repellent-tainted sweat from my eyes with the soaking wet bandana I held in my left hand, my right one fully occupied holding a cheap Russian-made single-shot 12 gauge shotgun at the ready. Mind you, even though the monetary value of the weapon may have been low, the true treasure I held in my sweaty palm was in the names of my heroes that had already been carved into its stock by the few previous hunters who had successfully collected the rarest of all the antelope in Africa, a male Royal Antelope. Rex Baker, Bill Figge, and a couple other legends had been to this same jungle, although closer to the coast, only weeks before me and had been successful. However, there had been a few others who were not so fortunate and were not allowed to whittle their names into the walnut stock...

The hunt, in jungle forest as thick as the hair on a coon dog's back, is conducted in the western African nation of Ghana. My hosts on this adventure turned out to be uncountable colonies of stinging bright green ants, the usual assortment of cobras, vipers, and other nasty reptilian troublemakers, and more scorpions than the USA has upside-down house mortgages.

The really tough part of the hunt, though, is dealing with the heat and the *humidity!* Oh, Lord, the humidity! You would think

157

The Ghana jungle

that since the hunt is at night for these nocturnal pint-size prizes that the temperatures would drop to a civil level, but *noooooo*. On top of the heat from hell and the steam room humidity level, you pray that it will rain so that the leaf litter quiets down to a level somewhat quieter than walking on cornflakes as you skitter after the tiny treasures. The rain, of course, sends the humidity to new, unfathomable levels, not fit for habitation by a scrawny white guy from Seattle, I can tell you.

I really don't know how they actually measure humidity, nor do I care, but we have all heard percentages sensually cooed to us across the airwaves (or I suppose nowadays across the cable lines) by some sexy blond weather wench gleefully telling us, "Today, expect partly cloudy skies, temperatures in the high 80s with 70 percent humidity throughout the weekend," or something similar.

Some kind of damn snake

So, using Al Smith's, not-so-factual calculations and calibrations, based on no scientific quantum theories whatsoever other than my firm belief in simple logic, I would assume that 100 percent humidity is liquid; i.e., if you tested a glass of icy-cold Pabst Blue Ribbon beer that it would register on whatever gauge the weather geeks use as being 100 percent humidity. Conversely, if you applied the same scale when measuring the red sand of the Mojave Desert at noon on the Fourth of July, it would register 0 percent humidity.

I have no idea if my assumptions are correct, but *work with me here, people,* and I hope you get where I'm going with this. Using these scientifically never-been-peer-group-reviewed calibrations of mine, the jungles of Ghana during the rainy season would be 99 percent relative humidity on the Smith Scale. Now that, my North American living-above-the-Mason-Dixon-Line friends, is HUMID!

The Safari Club International Record Book only contained five entries for Royal Antelope when I hunted there, and the last one entered had been in 1986, so you can see what a rare treat it was to be able to hunt these Chihuahua-sized creatures with inch-and-a-quarter-length horns.

To the uninitiated, the thought of pursuing the Tiny Titans of the African continent, and there are a multitude of different species of the little antelope and duikers, may seem like a waste of time and effort compared to hunting the glamorous Big Five, or sheep and goat hunting in Russia or Asia, or the mighty brown bears of Alaska, but I'm hear to tell you, brother, if you haven't done it, don't knock it 'til you try it.

Hunting any of the pygmy antelope can be extremely tough, with luck playing a much greater role in your success at acquiring one than many of their larger-horned cousins. As an example, I went on three 21-day trips to Tanzania before I was finally able to collect an East African duiker, which are fairly common. The little buggers never stand still long enough to get a shot, whereas I killed sable, roan, oryx, and a multitude of other larger target types of creatures there on the first day we tried for them. I had to kill both the Kirk's and the Guenther's dik-dik with my .375 H&H because I was only able to stumble onto them while chasing bigger game and not during the frustrating days of sneaky-sneaking through the thickets with the camp .22, intentionally hunting for them.

Luckily for the taxidermy world's sake, the Barnes Triple-Shock bullets I use fly through the little fellas like a solid, barely leaving more than a dime-sized hole on exiting. Keep in mind that 90 percent of the time you are on a mixed-bag safari you will be packing a high-powered rifle, so shooting at these nervous, poodle-sized buggers can be a real challenge, since hitting such a tiny target is virtually impossible under the best of circumstances.

Patiently calling blue duiker and yellow-backed duiker in the jungles of Central Africa is a different mind game of its own as these members of the fraternity charge toward the wailing call, zigzagging through the jungle, only to dash away at any sign of movement as you raise the shotgun to finish him off at 10 yards. It can quite often take days—or weeks—to be successful. Many a hunter has failed to connect on all the available duikers in Cameroon and the Central African Republic after 3 weeks of vigorous efforts.

In a nutshell, the little ungulates are a very worthy adversary to any Nimrod willing to go to the ends of the Dark Continent to fill out his collection, and the Royal Antelope of Ghana is unquestionably the toughest one I had ever run across, up to this point.

Tweek Roodt, my trusty young professional hunter on this adventure, and I finished another quart of water infused with Cytomax energy additive, while Asari, our 4-foot-6-inch tall semi-pygmy former poacher-turned guide had a small sip from his water bottle.

The two of us white guys looked as if we'd been standing under a shower for an hour fully clothed. Sweat continued to ooze from every pore, even while we rested. The humidity was draining us physically as well as mentally.

This short break from crawling for hours under thornbushes and fighting off stinging ants dropping down inside of our shirt collars from the overhanging limbs gave me a chance to ask Tweek if he knew the definition of relative humidity. Wondering, in his youthful innocence, what this had to do with anything related to royal antelope hunting, but humoring me, the paying client, he took the bait and said he did not.

"That's the sweat that builds up on your upper lip when you are making love to your cousin," I replied straight-faced.

While an oldie, but still a goody, it cracked the two of us up and lightened the rather dismal moment, considering we were on night 10 of a 10-day hunt, it was midnight, and there was no way I could extend my hunt any longer due to more pressing concerns back in the States, *called making a living so that I can keep hunting,* and we had yet to kill a male royal.

We were getting close to that stage one might call desperate and the severe conditions were not helping our attitudes. I looked over at Asari, finding perverse pleasure in the fact that he seemed to finally be breaking a sweat after the last several hours of stalking in the dark.

The technique for hunting the royals is pretty basic at first blush: You simply follow a local man through the jungle in the pitch-black darkness with a red-lens-colored headlamp on your forehead while he shines a flashlight to and fro until he sees the reflection of an antelope's eyes. He freezes when he sees the bluish reflection of their corneas and points with his finger where you should shoot. There are a couple of issues with this technique, however, that throw the proverbial monkey wrench into the equation.

One is, when the light hits the antelope in the eyes, he immediately turns his head away, making it impossible for you, the hunter, who is three steps behind the guide, to see the reflection of the animal's eyes when Asari freezes and points.

Second, the jungle is so thick you can't see the animal through the leaves and branches even if the eye threw a reflection.

Third, and most important, royals do not get "frozen in the headlights," as, say, a whitetail deer in Kansas would, and flee almost immediately after turning their heads. I was lucky in that a couple of my aforementioned friends had been to the dance before me and recommended bringing along a red dot laser pointer and training Asari on how to use it. This had the intended effect of him using the red dot to indicate where to shoot instead of pointing his tiny bony finger. That way, you only had to shoot at the red dot placed where he saw the antelope about to break for cover.

Problem number four is you have to stay right on the little Ghanese guide's shirttails all the time, otherwise the royal vanishes before you catch up to your guide once he locates it. At least I had the 5-foot-8-inch advantage of being able to stay fairly close to pee-wee Asari, whereas poor Tweek, at 6-foot-2-plus, was on his knees trying to follow us through thickets that would have made Brer Rabbit feel safe.

As Tweek stuffed the empty water jugs back into his pack, he looked at his watch in the glow of his red headlamp and said, "Alain, it's 1:30. I'll keep going as long as want. We have to be on the road by 8:30 at the latest, if you are going to catch your plane for home. What do you think?"

The last thing I wanted to do was go home without a Royal Antelope. I was very concerned that Ghana may not even be open for hunting again next year. I knew Steve Kobrine, the bow-hunting maniac and booking agent who had successfully opened the country up for other hunters, had spent years getting things started and that all it would take is one change in political attitudes in the Ghana government or some not-so-subtle pressure from the anti-hunters at the World Bank or the IMF and that would be the end of my chance for a royal. So all we could do was keep going to the very last minute and hope the jungle-hunting spirits would look favorably upon my suspect soul.

I replied to Tweek, "Why don't we try along the bigger pathways and get out of the thick stuff? I think we are making too much noise crashing through the tangles, and it's too thick to see anything anyhow where we've been hunting so far."

Plus it will be a hell of a lot easier walking, I thought, but didn't verbalize.

"I'm with you on that," Tweek agreed. "We can make a big swing around where we've been and slowly work our way back to the truck. My guess is we are still an hour and a half from it."

Tweek translated through a few basic words and lots of point-ing and miming to Asari what our intentions were. Asari nodded in agreement, before turning and starting down the well-beaten path we were resting on.

The little man only walked 50 yards before turning back into the thick crap once again, hunting by the same method as he had been for the past week. At first, I assumed he had a shortcut in mind, until I realized he had not caught the gist of Tweek's remonstrations.

Not willing to crawl much further, I was able to catch up to him and grab hold of his filthy T-shirt, getting his attention. He didn't want to go back to the trail, so I simply tugged long enough that he frustratedly worked his way back to the path, muttering to himself a litany of not-so-complementary views as to our intended plan.

Now Tweek demonstrated to him how to walk slowly and check out all the thick spots from the main path. I could see by his sour attitude that he did not like our idea but reluctantly he began to comply. A couple more tugs as he would venture off the beaten path and we were soon all working off the same page.

I could feel my attention span fading as we trudged along the vine-choked path, keeping an eye out for more snakes and running quickly away every time Asari did, which meant he had stepped in another pile of stinging ants. A guy can only pack so much opti-mism into one night, and I have to admit, my positive attitude well had gone dry. I was dripping wet with sweat. Even pouring water over my face didn't refresh me as it had earlier in the night, and I figured we had finally run out of luck on this trip.

I had just looked up from my depressed stupor to see what Asari was doing an arm's length in front of me, when he froze and to my utter disbelief, pointed the laser pointer 10 yards off to my right. In one fluid motion, the safety clicked off, I swung the bar-rel of the single-shot to the right, and found the minute laser dot wavering on some unseen target. Trusting Asari's eyes more than mine, I pulled the trigger, setting off a cloud of dust, foggy vapor, and branches while falling leaves filled the air from the shock of the shot. I quickly reloaded the single-shot break-open action as Asari knelt down staring off to our left and pointing at the fleeing royal. I saw him disappear with a limp into the jungle...

Tweek came alongside of me and asked what happened.

"I hit him, but I don't know how good. I saw him limping but still going pretty good off that way," I said pointing to my left.

"Let's fan out and see if we can find him," Tweek responded. "He's got to be here somewhere. See if you can find any blood. Did you reload?"

"I'm ready," I said as I took up the trail, each one of us scanning the area with our Sure-Fire flashlights to aid our fading headlamps.

After 10 minutes, we had found nothing, and if I could have kicked myself in my own testicles, I would have for missing the little target. No blood, only the tracks where he ran for the first 20 yards, and then his track disappeared in the dense leafy floor of the jungle.

Tweek continued to search on my left, and Asari had disappeared to my right when I heard a distinct whistle that didn't belong in this dark jungle. I looked to my right and saw Asari's headlamp blinking on and off at me, signaling to me.

I ran as fast as I could, getting ripped up pretty good in the process as I made my way to where he crouched. When he saw me, he simply smiled and pointed with the laser pointer into the thickest part of the jungle where I could barely make out a tiny leg below a platter-sized round green leaf. I held just above the leg where the body should be and let the number four pellets do their assigned duty. When the mist and dust settled, there lay my prize, a little shot up, but salvageable and dead!

Asari and I with my trophy Royal

It was a long but joyous trek back to the truck with a couple hours to spare before our long drive back to Accra where my airplane home should be waiting. At the truck, Tweek and I pampered ourselves and toasted each other's manliness with a lukewarm, but wet, beer, one that contained 100 percent humidity, just like my clothes...

Asari, the reformed poacher

Larry the Cable Guy's Hat

ONE OF THE BEST things about going to the Safari Club International's Convention located in Reno, Nevada, most years is going to the evening entertainment. Such celebs as Dana Carvey, both George Bush's, the Beach Boys, Tom Selleck, and Jim Belushi, just to name a few, have graced the stage at the annual event held over 4 days.

In 2011, the Wednesday night attraction was the one and only Larry the Cable Guy. Now, if there was ever someone who was playing to his kind of crowd, it was certainly Larry this night, entertaining a room of 3,000 hunters, with more than two-thirds of them being rednecks, whether or not they want to admit it.

While some of his potty humor may have offended a small percentage of the Bible-beater faction in attendance, the remainder of the crowd was either trying to hide the fact that they were cracking up to the redneck jokester or howling in the aisles.

At the conclusion of his act (which he extended and ad-libbed for the last 20 minutes), Larry The Cable Guy took off his camo baseball hat with the signature fishing hook clipped onto the bill and gave it a Frisbeelike toss into the crowd, the lucky recipient of the treasure being my tablemate and hunting companion Dennis Anderson.

Besides being a past president of SCI, Dennis was at the time of the aforementioned comedy show the president of the Hunter Legacy Fund, a group of hunters who contributed substantial funds to a foundation that disburses the earnings from the fund to worthy conservation programs around the world. He also plays an active role in raising funds for the SCI-PAC political action arm of Safari Club each year, so when the present from Larry ended up in his lap, he looked across the dinner table at me and mouthed the words, "I'm going to auction this off at SCI-PAC."

What a wonderful thing to do for conservation and protecting hunters' rights, I thought, as I choked down the rest of my mystery meat dinner.

As luck would have it, I found myself at the SCI-PAC lunch that Saturday, listening to an extremely inspiring speech by Michael Reagan, son of the greatest U.S. president ever, Ronald Reagan, followed up by an auction to raise much-needed money for political action and candidates that support our hunting heritage.

I will be the first to admit that like the majority of men, most of my purchases at auctions revolve around several factors: a good cause, a good-looking woman displaying the auction item, and alcohol, not necessarily in that order...

Since Dennis was the stand-in auctioneer for the first few items at the SCI-PAC auction and it was only lunchtime, two of my three main reasons for donating were not covered. Good thing it was a good cause, then, eh?

First item up on the auction block was Larry's cap, and Dennis gave a rundown to the crowd as to whose head the camo hunting hat had graced and the fact that he had had the hat personally autographed by Larry, sending a murmur of approval throughout the packed auditorium, before explaining how the bidding was going to work on the celebrity chapeau.

"All right," he rattled into the microphone, "here's how this is going to work. It's like a poker game. Once you bid on the hat, your money is in the kitty and it doesn't come out. This isn't like a normal auction 'cause this is a special item. Everybody understand?"

Nodding heads were seen around the room as people comprehended that if they bid and someone else raised the bid, their money still stayed in and they would have to pay up, whether or not they got the hat.

"OK, let's go. Who will make the first bid?" Dennis yelled, looking around the hall for the first hand to go up. Hesitation held court until Mr. Anderson, in his not-so-subtle-way, looked over at my table in the front of the room with a devilish grin and an I've-got-you-now smile, and said, "All right, Alain Smith is in for the opening bid of $5,000."

Since there is not much you can do when you are put in the spotlight in front of your peers by a so-called good friend, I, of course, laughed and nodded in agreement to the deal. Dennis then proceeded to work the room and raise more and more money from his friends and fellow patriots, including Ralph and Debbie Cunningham and family, members of Dennis Anderson's family, and Stan and Pamela Atwood's family members, just to name a few.

About this time, and certainly feeling like I had done *my* part, Dennis decided he had not quite raised enough dough for the cause and began working yours truly over once again. Deciding two can play this game, I upped the ante by stating to the crowd and our illustrious auctioneer when he cornered me once again, "I'll tell you what I'll do. I'll raise the bid, but for that, you have to wear the Larry The Cable Guy hat in all the pictures we take on our upcoming trip to Pakistan next week." That brought lots of laughs and reversed the pressure back to Dennis, who, of course, reluctantly agreed to the deal, to the howling delight of the assembled hunters.

"Is that it?" Dennis begged into the mike. "Somebody else save me from this fate, please. Come on, Stan and Pam, are you going to let Alain do this to me?" he joked, trying to put some pressure on them as well.

Now, one thing I have learned in the years I have known the Atwoods is you better be careful if you are going to challenge them, and now, they rose to the occasion for a good cause. Pamela looked at Stan with a searching gaze, then turned back and yelled out, "We raise the bid again, and you still have to wear the hat for the Pakistan pictures, only now, you have to turn it sideways when you take them, and then you have to bring the hat back after the hunt and give it to me for the grandkids."

That set the crowd laughing and razzing Dennis, who, once again, agreed to the final terms.

When the smoke finally cleared and it was all said and done, the total raised from the auctioning of the hat by all the very generous families who attended the SCI-PAC lunch was $67,500. Wow! Now it was time for the second leg of the bid and for Dennis to fulfill his end of the deal.

Some 59 hours of flying, driving, flying some more, four-wheel driving, with only 6 of those hours spent in a bed and only a week after the SCI convention, found Dennis and I unpacking our luggage in the Torghar Mountains of western Pakistan for our hunt after the elusive Afghan urial.

The weather was a little dicey for the typically hot, dry, semi-desert mountains, rain being rarer than Christians in this part of the world. However, during our first 2 days there, both visited the Torghars. Rain not being very conducive to successful sheep hunting, we struck out the first couple days. However, day 3 dawned clear and cold, holding promise that today was the day.

After a 2-hour, bone-jarring rough ride from camp and 2 hours of climbing up a dry riverbed, we found ourselves nestled into a promontory where we could see for miles in any direction. Our guides from Shikar Safaris, Sarp and Serkan, who had made all the arrangements for the trip, translated to us that the guides wanted to sit and glass from here because there were sheep hiding in the nooks and crannies below and when the sun came above the horizon, we would surely see sheep.

It was Dennis's turn as the shooter so I helped glass and used the built-in range finder on my Leica binoculars to test the distances involved. No matter where a wily ram stuck his head out below us, no shot would be less than 250 yards, and my guess, which I related to Dennis, was that any shot would be .350-ish, so get ready for that kind of shot.

We hadn't been at our perch for more than a couple of hours when one of the local guides spotted a small band of sheep with one respectable ram in the bunch, working their way toward us from a deep chasm to our right. They meandered along toward us, browsing at scrub brush, enjoying the sun's warming rays until halfway to our appointed rendezvous location, when the herd of urials veered slightly left.

"They are going to that tree there on the horizon," whispered the old silver-haired guide.

Dennis got set up with a good rest, his pack cushioning his pride and joy, a well broken-in Weatherby .30-378. Undoubtedly that caliber is perhaps a little "overkill" on an 80-pound sheep, but the weapon is specifically designed for long-range shooting and thank God it is, since my range finder read the distance to the lone tree the band of sheep were heading toward as being 458 yards! Now I've seen my buddy Dennis make some miraculous shots, but this one was semistretching the limits of physics at a very small target.

The urials did just as the guide predicted, walking up the mountain and stopping under the shade of the lone tree. Dennis said, "Plug your ears. I'm going to shoot."

Those who didn't do as instructed were staggered by the blast from the muzzle brake as the 180 grain bullet was sent on its deadly mission, hitting the ram a little too far back in the guts but raking forward into the boiler room. The ram unbelievably absorbed the shot and staggered further up the mountain another 100 yards before disappearing over the crest.

High fives were slapped all around in that awkward way that only old white guys and Pakistani tribesmen can do. Everyone was positive that the ram was down. Sure enough, an hour later, after a breakneck hike to the last place we saw the sheep disappear, the ram was found deader than Senator John Kerry's odds of getting elected as president of the USA.

What a shot!

Of course, the glamour pictures were taken of this very difficult animal to collect and being the good sport he is, Larry The Cable

Dennis and Sarp with a great Blandford urial he also took on this trip

Guy's hat was reverently placed upon Dennis's cranium per the final requirements of Pam and Stan's donation. Dennis continued his hunt in Southern Pakistan, in the Dureji region, and took several other outstanding trophies, the hat making all the pictures.

We are all very lucky to be able to hunt and fish in this great country of ours, as well as exotic places like Pakistan, and thanks to SCI-PAC's efforts and individuals willing to put their hard earned money toward causes we all believe in, *while having a lot of fun in the process*, hopefully, our children and grandchildren will be able to do the same.

A pair of Sindh ibex from Dureji and the hat

Jaguar

THE ADVENTURE BEGAN WITH a phone call from the manager of a remote lodge, asking Rocky if he could fly up and capture a jaguar that had caused a little "mayhem," shall we say, at the vast estancia he oversaw, located along the swamps of the Paraguay/Brazilian border.

Seems Mr. Spots had become so embolden that the night before the manager called, the bold jaguar had broken through the wire mesh bug screen surrounding the lodge's decks and strode nonchalantly up the stairs to the second floor where the cook and her 10-year-old son worked on the evening meal. The family mongrel lay in the luxurious living room grooming himself, licking his lower extremities, [because he can] when El Tigre pounced on the unsuspecting mutt, breaking its neck in one bone-crunching bite behind the ears.

Paying no attention to the screaming woman sheltering her child behind her, the cat simply carried the easy meal back out the new hole in the screening and trotted off into the jungle.

The camp manager proffered the cost of the relocation and any other expenses, but insisted that Rocky come right away. Rocky broached the subject at dinner to my hunting partner, renowned surgeon Dr. Doug Yajko, and me.

"So that's the story, gents," Rocky completed the tale. "Doug, can you wait here at the farm and continue hunting some deer,

177

The lodge that the jaguar broke into

capybara, and caiman while I take Alain to the other place with me? We can't all get in the plane with the dogs and gear, and since you already darted a jaguar earlier in the week..."

"No problem. I'll hold the fort down with your crew here," Dr. Doug replied, relieved, I'm sure, that he didn't have to go through another jungle chase through the vegetative hell that is the Paraguayan lowlands.

The next morning as the bloodred sun snuck over the eastern horizon, we were airborne in the still morning air, gliding above the green canopy, belted in to Rocky's 182 Cessna. A whiff of rotten eggs, mixed with a sulfuric 10-day-old gut pile suddenly engulfed the tin coffin we were trapped in. I cranked my head to blame the gaseous stench on Rocky, but changed my mind when he began to wretch, his face contorted in a scowl that would scare the hood off the Grim Reaper. He immediately stared back at me accusatorily.

Doug's cat with a couple of darts in him

Dr. Doug Yajko, Rocky McBride, and a local guide with Doug's jaguar

"Hey...that wasn't me," I countered looking back over my shoulder at the old Plott hound, lounging on the backseat, while his two sons by different mothers lay curled up on the floor. I swear to God, I saw that old mutt grin as he opened one eye to see what all the commotion was about in the front seats. Since you can't open the window at 3,500 feet going 130 miles per hour, we toughed it out, gagging each time one of the cat chasers crepitated.

"Guess I should have let them run around a little more," was all Rocky could say during the remainder of the 2-hour flight to the Pantanal.

"So this very wealthy American heiress bought the 260,000-acre ranch we are going to, setting up a conservancy to protect it forever," Rocky filled me in as we began approaching the vast estate.

"It's mostly swamp and flood plain, but is home to a tremendous variety of wildlife, especially birds, many of which are only found in this area. Her main interest is the hyacinth macaw, which flourish in this remote area, and she wants to protect them. There is no road to the ranch. Everything must be flown in or brought up the Piranha River by small boat.

"You'll see the beautiful lodge she had built here for scientists and students to stay at while they study the area. These folks are doing good things for wildlife, and they are not antihunters. I spoke to the owner on the phone last night, and she would prefer that we capture and move the jaguar and not kill it if possible. I told her we would. Funny thing though, the woman who owns this place has never been here."

I let that sink in as we descended toward the dirt landing strip carved out of the palm trees, standing like sentinels waiting for the next flood. Flocks of snowy white egrets, uncountable doves, and Jacarra rose from the edges of the strip as we bounced gently to a stop in the yard of the estancia. None of the three dogs made it more than a hundred feet from the plane before they assumed the position.

We ate, fed the dogs, and hit the sack, not long after sundown.

"What the hell..."

I woke from another restless sweaty sleep, confused by the rum ruminating in my fevered brain, annoyed by the high-pitched jabbering Spanish just outside my room.

"*Onca, Onca! Senor, El Tigre es aqui. Come rapido. Señor!*"

Through the verbal fog I caught Rocky McBride's Texas-tainted Español from the room next door.

"*Sí, sí, uno momento.*" Then as if I needed a nudge he yelled over to me, "Alain, get your clothes on. The jaguar is outside!" I had comprende'd enough of the exchange to already have my pants pulled on by the time Rocky barked his instructions through the lodge's thin mahogany walls.

The dogs started howling at the top of their lungs now that the scent of the cat wafted through the screened-in porch where they had been sleeping. The pitch of the three cat hounds climbed to Marshall amp volume as Rocky yelled, "They can see him. Hear that? He's just outside the lodge. Let's go!"

We met on the veranda outside our rooms a moment later, Rocky armed with a dart rifle, me with a .357 Smith and Wesson pistol tucked not so discreetly in my belt.

"Here, hold this," Rocky said, handing me the rifle as he opened his plastic tackle box that had been converted into a portable medicine chest, filled with various-sized darts and pharmaceuticals intended to send big kitties into la-la land when sent flying from the rifle I held. Not sure what the plan was and too afraid to ask such a stupid question at this juncture of the night, I glanced at my watch, noting the four o'clock position of Mickey's hands.

"Let's see if we can sneak around the other side of the lodge and you can stick him in the hind end with this dart. Remember, he has to be inside 20 yards for this rifle to be really accurate."

Rocky handed me the red-tailed dart he had filled with enough ketamine to slow the jaguar down, so I eased the silver cylinder very carefully into the breach. Pricking one's finger with the concoction would surely have a worse effect on my dancing ability than the rum had the night before.

The hounds were still sounding off, leaping into the mesh mosquito screen, trying anything to get at their adversary, who, we would soon find out, was dragging a young Brahman calf through the backyard, looking for a more tranquil place to dine, as we snuck down the stairs and around the front of the lodge attempting to cut him off before he slipped back into the dense jungle.

Perhaps if the ranch manager would have shut up and quit yelling from the safety of his second-story front porch or perhaps if the three dogs had not been going completely bonkers as we snuck around the corner of the building, I would have got a shot at El Tigre, as the locals called him, but no luck tonight. He had vanished with his fresh bovine breakfast into the encroaching jungle.

"Let's go back in the house and get some coffee and breakfast and wait till dawn to follow that jaguar," Rocky said as I stood next to the lodge wondering what we were going to do now that the cat had vanished with the calf into the pitch-black darkness.

"He won't go far with that young calf before he starts eating him."

No better idea had ever revealed itself to me up to that moment, I thought as I poured a cup of thick Paraguayan joe. I had wrestled too much with the jaguar. Dr. Doug had stuck a dart in a few days earlier when the drugs had not been strong enough to put him under and the damn thing had given us fits when we tried to hold him down so Rocky could give him another dose. So the

What was left of the calf

thought of doing something similar, only in the dark, ranked up there with swimming naked in the Piranha River, trolling for its toothy namesakes.

At dawn, Josélito, the ranch capo, met us outside the lodge with three trusty steeds, saddled and jittery. The nags were of surprisingly good stock for out here in the middle of nowhere and handled well as we left the corrals on a trail carved out of the miserable jungle. I tore my pant leg on the first brush we passed, the horse not paying attention, nor was I up until then, but I did from then on. I pulled at the dozen thorns hooked into my knee, wiping the trickle of blood away before anyone else saw it.

Josélito reined in his horse not a hundred yards from the house, dismounting and staring at the ground next to the trail. Suddenly, his mount let out a frightened whinny before the brushy thicket

Caballero

15 yards in front of us exploded, setting all three horses into a mild panic. Me too...

Rocky handed me his reins after he dismounted so I could keep his prancing steed under control while he reconnoitered the area.

Crawling into the thorny thicket on his hands and knees, he looked back over his shoulder toward me and quietly filled us in. "The calf, or what's left of it, is right here. The jaguar was here when we rode up. That was him we heard run off. By the looks of the tracks, he's a real monster. Wow."

Back to lodge we rode for new supplies, where Rocky filled me in about what to expect next as we loaded a couple backpacks with assorted goodies.

"I'm sure the brute will come back to the calf. He's not afraid of humans; hell, he might not have ever seen one living out here in the swamp. Our best bet is going to be trying to trap him. I don't like this setup for running the dogs. It's too swampy, and the cat will bay on one of the small islands, and when he does, he'll wait for the dogs and kill them all. They won't have a chance against a cat this size in the thickets of these little dry spots. I've trapped them before. This'll work."

Rocky stuffed a brace of rubber-jawed leg hold traps that his family designed and manufactures into his weathered rucksack, along with the assorted accoutrements needed for the task ahead, and then we hiked back to the Brahman calf carcass.

Setting a trap, *a trap that will catch something,* is an art form, and as I watched this Texan Michelangelo dig a shallow hole, place the steel trap, set it, and camouflage the immediate area with the skill of a true Renaissance man, my confidence swelled. If the cat came back, and Rocky said he would, this jaguar was going to meet Mr. Jaws and end his cattle killing days once and for all.

"Let's go back to the lodge and get some lunch. He should be back later in the afternoon," Rocky whispered as we backed out of the tangled thorny thicket, before dodging our way through the rapierlike thorns for 10 minutes, back to the safety of the lodge.

If you have never experienced a siesta after getting up at o'dark thirty, working your buns off all morning in staggering heat and humidity, followed by a big lunch chased with a couple of icy-cold beers, you haven't lived. I woke from my midday fantasy-filled dreams, then freshened up with a quick shower before heading downstairs to find Rocky speaking with the lodge manager.

"It's a little early, but I think we should check the trap. I don't want Mr. Spots tangled up in that trap too long. He might hurt himself. You ready to go, Sleeping Beauty?"

"*Sí, vamanos,* " I replied for the Spanish-speaking manager's enjoyment.

As we closed to within 50 yards of the thicket that held the trap, Rocky began to stealthily sneak on the side of his weathered boots. I followed his lead while cradling the dart gun in the crook of my right arm. Easing onto our hands and knees, we crawled into the dimly lit tangle peering ahead for any sign of the cat.

Suddenly, Rocky froze, staring straight-ahead at what I soon focused on as well. The spotted *gato* lay staring back at us 20 yards away, snarling, showing us his fangs, telling us in no uncertain terms to not come any closer. Rocky brought his binos up to get a closer look at how the cat was caught in the trap but was having trouble in the gray light focusing. I slipped up next to him hoping to stick a dart in the jaguar when suddenly the cat vanished into the enveloping jungle.

"Damn it," Rocky hissed. "He didn't step in a trap. Let's take a look and see what's up." Making our way one slow crawling knee at a time, not wanting to provoke a charge if the cat decided to defend his kill, we finally saw that the neither of the two traps had been sprung. Rocky silently pointed out where the tracks showed the paws had barely missed stepping on the trigger plate discreetly hidden below some scattered leaves and sand. Rocky pulled some broken branches from the creeper vines to form a more restrictive tunnel leading to the calf carcass, forcing Mr. Spots to walk onto one of the traps.

"Let's go back to the lodge, rest a while, and see if he'll come back," whispered my guide.

Soaking wet from a potent concoction of heat, humidity, and fear, we worked our way back to the two-story structure keeping our fingers crossed that we'd get another crack at the cat.

"If we see him again, stick a dart in him right away, OK, Alain?"

"Sure. Hand me that extra dart just in case," I whispered back as we crawled closer an hour and a half later.

"Don't prick yourself with that thing," Rocky smiled as he handed me a freshly loaded silver dart of kitty Ambien. Taking heed, I very carefully placed the projectile in the left breast pocket of my khaki shirt.

We both secured headlamps to our dripping foreheads before assuming the crawling position once again. The barrel of the pistol stung my hip as I bent over, lodged as it was, tight in my belt, the shiny foot-long knife strapped to my calf. I'm telling you, Rambo had nothin' on me.

It was almost completely dark as we slipped in on the now-familiar trail toward the baby Brahman's fly-covered remains. Rocky kept his SureFire flashlight turned off until arriving in the pitch-black darkness at the location where we had spotted the cat at earlier. He squeezed my arm in the prearranged signal that now was the time to flick on our headlamps.

The blinding illumination stunned my senses momentarily until I felt the eyes of the jaguar staring menacingly back at us 20 yards ahead. As I raised the dart gun, checking the pressure gauge to make sure it would have enough power to reach the cat, Rocky flipped on his handheld torch, flooding the cat with enough light to get a better look at the situation.

The cat lay half-hidden behind the carcass, snarling at us, his massive bloody muzzle twitching nervously. Thoughts of running as fast as I could back to the lodge teased my paranoid-filled cranium as I locked into a shooting position with only a very tight shot through the tangle of branches and leaves between me and El Tigre. The 5 seconds it took the jumbo jaguar to rise up, giving me some fur to shoot at, seemed like hours as I began to question my sanity at pursuing this venture any further.

"Now," Rocky hissed at the same moment I squeezed the trigger, sending the dart in a shimmering arc dead center into the monster's chest. The jungle erupted, coming alive as the cat let out a pain-filled feline scream, biting at the dart dangling from his massive chest, before spinning on his heels and disappearing into the black jungle.

"Nice shot, amigo. Now we need to put another one in him before he goes too far. That one will only slow him down. Wait here. I'm going to go get some dogs," Rocky said as he hurried back to the lodge.

I sat in the dark, alone with my prayers, and hope that the cat had not gone too far. I had honestly forgot it takes two darts' worth of ketamine to put the jaguar down and knew we still had lots of excitement left in our bag of fun this evening.

I flipped my light off, *saving batteries*, I told myself, but hoping that the jaguar wouldn't see me sitting there in the thicket, all alone...just me and my Bowie knife and my pistol. My stomach growled in nervous protest at the circumstances as Rocky showed up with a bigger light and Cody, the young hound, tugging at his leash.

"I'm going to keep him on the leash to track the cat. He won't be able to fight it single-handedly. You ready, compadre?"

"Yep, I put the extra charge in the rifle. You sure about all this?" I questioned.

"Yeah, we'll get him. The drugs will have kicked in by now."

Rocky missed the point of what I asked (or maybe he was just ignoring it), so we began to follow the jaguar's scent, Cody howling as he walked up to the calf's carcass sucking full nostrils of onca odor. The big dog lunged at the end of the lead, trying to break free, not used to being held back when he was this close to his quarry. Rocky held on tight as the hound sang out. I could hear his two kennel mates back at the house joining in on the chorus, yelping in harmony, trying to join in on the chase.

Rocky picked his way through the tangled web of thorns, hacking at it with his machete, clearing what he could as fishhook thorns dug deep into our flesh. I carried the rifle at the ready position, my left hand holding the pistol and the forestock of the dart gun simultaneously, swinging the business end from side to side, expecting a flurry of spotted fury to be all over my former-Canadian carcass any minute now. As we waded across a small creek, the reflection of devilish yellow eyes flickered in the beam of light from Rocky's flashlight.

"There, stick another one in him," Rocky urged me on. The light bounced around as the fearless dog was now going completely beserko at the sight of the doped-up monster so close.

As El Gato stood to escape from his drugged sitting position, I was able to hit him again, this time closer to the tail. Biting at his derriere, the cat spun in a circle for a few seconds. I dropped the rifle and held the pistol out in front of me like a cop busting into a room filled with bank robbers, praying that the cat would not realize who had stung him in the ass, wishing I were invisible. It did not take more than 3 or maybe 4 minutes tops for the cat to settle down, giving in to the pharmaceutical bliss of the drugs, sitting down on his haunches, taking one last look in my direction before laying his head on his massive paws and passing out.

As we slowly approached, the jaguar's enormity became readily apparent.

"Damn, that is a big son-of-a-bitch," Rocky drawled. "Let's get a couple quick pictures, and then we have to get to work on him."

The hordes of mosquitoes found that while I crouched down for the glamour shots, I made an outstanding target for their own dart guns. The jungle juice I had smeared over my exposed skin earlier did nothing to deter them as the little vermin ate me alive while I smiled for the camera.

Rocky put the camera back in his pack and dug out a scale, tracking collar, and sample vile. We measured the monster, finding him to weigh 242 pounds, huge by any standards, while his length of 8 foot 6 inches, combined with the circumference of his head and chest, totaled 156? inches, making him the biggest jaguar ever darted and measured for the record books.

The business end of an old gato

Rocky secured a radio transmitting collar on the cat, having to punch a couple new holes in the strap because the massive neck wouldn't accept the typical hole pattern used on other jaguars.

"What are we going to do with him now?" I asked, wiping Off-tainted sweat from my brow as I stood, feeling the ache throb in my sports-ruined knees.

A real monster of a cat

"Let's drag him out of here to where we can get the Jeep to him, and then we'll load him in the plane and haul him to the park. There's an airstrip there that I can land on," Rocky casually quipped.

"Say what?" I uttered.

"Yeah, you get in the backseat with the onca and if he starts to wake up, give him some more drugs and he'll fall back asleep."

The thought of me and 242 pounds of pent-up fury waking up at 3,000 feet elevation sounded immediately like a reeeaaallly bad idea.

"I know how to fly your plane, Rocky. How about you get in the backseat with El Tigre and I'll fly the plane and keep the pistol up front with me as a *safety measure?*"

"He is pretty damn big. It might be tough getting him in the backseat, now that you mention it...Let's take him in the boat

Rocky bolting on a radio collar

instead, and we'll run him downriver far enough that he'll hopefully not come back here and harass the staff and their cattle. If he does, I'm sure they won't put up with it and will shoot him next time they see him, so we need to get him far enough away."

So we did.

I could tell you about the decision-making process running through my mind as the flat-bottom riverboat sped down the greasy black river in the moonlit darkness and I patted the Bowie knife and pistol strapped to my side as a confidence builder.

If El Gato wakes up and the knockout medicine shot doesn't take effect right away, do I jump in the river and take my chances with the piranhas, black caiman, and 20-foot long anaconda we saw on the bank of the river earlier, or do I tough it out and hope I am quicker at getting to the bow of the boat than Rocky is?

But I won't...

Ibex Don't Get Any Respect

I F THERE WAS EVER an animal that doesn't get the respect it deserves, it would have to be ibex. Talk about the redheaded stepchild of mountain animals! These crafty critters of the crags and crevices have taken a backseat to their *Ovis* neighbors long enough. It's time to give them the credit they are due!

Perhaps some of their disrespect as top-tier trophy species comes from the fact that they are much less expensive to hunt than their sheep buddies. I don't know about your wallet's contents, but I like the idea of an "affordable" adventure, when compared to the budget-busting prices being charged for wild sheep hunts these days. For the price of one argali hunt, a guy can go shoot three different ibex and pay for his airfare and still have some change left over for a cocktail or two in the local pub.

Don't think that just 'cause they are cheaper, that the thrills of being in the mountains are any less exciting either; far from it. In most cases, the goats live in even more extreme terrain than sheep and tend to stay on the cliff faces all day, where access is limited to those Nimrods whose testicles are larger than their brains, and holding on for dear life, using your hands as much as your feet to climb, is an acceptable form of entertainment.

195

The only alternative to climbing, of course, is taking ridiculously long shots across windswept chasms in typically numbing temperatures, a miss equaling another dejected trip down the mountain, followed up by a new dawn of scratching your way to the top once again.

My first ibex was one of the Gobi variety, taken as an add-on to a Hanguy argali sheep hunt in the fabulous mountains surrounding the vast desert of Mongolia. I had been successful with the argali after only 6 days, leaving me time to pursue other species available on short notice. We moved our camp via antique Russian Jeeps to a series of canyons falling away from the barren Gobi desert.

Setting up a tent camp on a plateau a half mile from the edge of one of the major canyons, the fire the guides made that night from wood hauled in on top of the trucks was a welcome source of heat when the temperatures fell to near zero Fahrenheit.

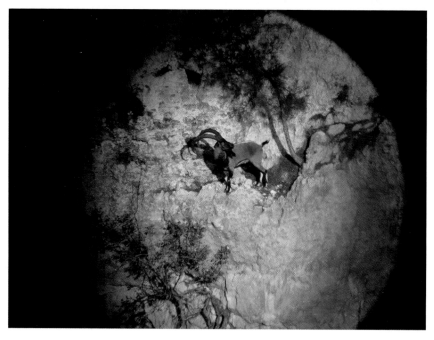

Bezoar ibex through the spotting scope

The guides, in traditional Mongolian fashion, spent most of the night celebrating our success with the argali, or whatever other excuse they could think of to have a party. The shindig was a doozy and at three in the morning when I got up to answer nature's call, I saw some of them, those that could still stand, whooping and hollering and staggering around the fire, warming their innards with copious amounts of Mongolian vodka.

Needless to say, the next morning was not a daybreak, up-and-at-'em affair, but I was able to get some hot water boiling for coffee after I rolled a couple of the guides who had not made it into their tents, away from the edge of the fire, noticing that the oldest guide had burnt the back of his coat from sleeping a little too close to the flames.

Three days of climbing down rocky chutes, mixed with glassing from the top of ridgelines and outcroppings, found us scoping out a herd of 2 dozen ibex with two decent males in their midst. The local domestic sheepherder-turned-guide took us on a circuitous route that brought the wind into our favor, allowing us to close the gap between our posse and the herd.

Sidehilling across steep loose shale, while trying to protect my brand-new rifle from damage each time I slipped and fell, took forever. The guides were not doing much better than I was at staying on their feet, so when we came up short of our prey, arriving at a sheer drop of several hundred feet and peeking over some boulders at the herd we were supposed to shoot at, milling about several hundred yards away, the head guide turned to me and intimated, "Time for you to shoot from here, dude."

I didn't have a range finder in those days, so all I knew was that the ibex were still what seemed to me to be a long, long ways off. To make matters worse, the herd became nervous and began to skip and climb away from us, gaining altitude on us with each step.

Having no choice but to give it a try, I found the biggest billy in the Zeiss scope, got comfortable in the rocks where I lay, and hoped the brute would stop skipping from rock to rock long enough for me to get a killing shot in on him.

I probably should confess here, that in those days of my rookie mountain hunting, I did not take the wind, angle of the shot, or exact distance into account, so when the ibex leapt up onto a huge boulder to get a better look back at us, Kentucky windage guestimating took over and I pulled the trigger, and surprise of all surprises, missed the damn thing. The good news was I missed over the top of the goat's back and a little to the right, so I made a quick adjustment, aiming lower and to the left, while the ibex looked back at the rocks where the first bullet had hit, wondering what the racket was all about. At the second report of the rifle, the Gobi ibex billy dropped dead, getting hung up in the smaller rocks below the boulder. I had taken my first ibex!

Now I will grant some of the skeptics out there that there are a few semieasy ibex one can hunt, such as the four Spanish ones, but even the term *semieasy* is relative when it comes to mountain hunting.

I was fortunate to hunt in Spain with guide-outfitter José Mallo for a couple of the Macho Montes as they are referred to in Española. We traveled by road from Madrid toward the Barcelona region, one of the haunts of the subspecies of Spanish ibex, the Beceite. I can't recall a more beautiful drive than the one from busy Madrid, winding through ancient farmlands with stone walls guiding you to the majestic mountains where the ibex are protected by the local villagers.

The typical Castilian village we arrived at, with its tall Catholic steeple overshadowing the rustic stone and brick buildings below, made for a tight squeeze on the skinny stone-paved streets designed 500 years earlier for horse-drawn carts, not José's four-wheel drive SUV.

*The final place a Southeastern ibex came to rest. This was supposed
to be an "easy" hunt?*

A meal fit for a king in the lonely massive dining room of the classy old hotel we shacked up in was complemented by the fabulous bottle of local Tempranillo wine José ordered from the cellar. A somewhat different start to an ibex hunt than staying in the tent, freezing my gluteus maximus off in Mongolia, one might say.

The hunting permits for this area are very tightly controlled with only three being issued by the local authorities per season, so it's a big event when someone comes to collect one of the coveted beasts. Most of the money from the permit fees goes to the local council, giving the villagers a real financial incentive to conserve the ibex. Everyone I met during my stay there was excited to have a hunter in town to collect one of their prized wild goats.

After meeting up with a couple of local guides an hour before dawn at the crest of a steep ridge, we all began to work our way in the dark down a loose rocky canyon, grabbing for handholds on the brush that sprouted out between the broken shale cliffs. The cloud cover wasn't providing us any help, hiding the moon and stars, none of us chancing using our flashlights that might scare any potential victims into the next county.

As the Iberian dawn gave us the chance to see what the surrounding hills might hold, we spied several bands of males sneaking in and out of the brush on the opposing hillsides, but according to my local guides, none were of the quality we had come so far to hunt.

Climbing back out of the canyon after scouring the area completely, we snuck from ridge top to ridge top, searching each canyon's sheer face for a big Beceite. While we saw plenty of ibex, and considering I had a week to hunt, we could afford to be picky as we scrambled about, the locals covering the well-worn cliffs as if they themselves were part goat.

After a *tapas* lunch on the side of the mountain under broken white clouds, the sun warming our cold bodies, the four of us sneaked in a great Spanish tradition, the siesta. When we woke, each one of us began gathering our gear while José put away the remains of our lunch in his pack.

Suddenly, one of the local guides hissed for all of us to freeze as he pointed off to our left at a band of ibex emerging from the brush 500 yards away, feeding unconcernedly toward where we lay hidden among some jagged rocks. Males were the predominant gender in this band of approximately 30 animals that picked at the bushes, browsing among the rocks while doing that "goat thing," climbing upon everything, surveying their domain, randomly head-butting each other, all the things that ibex love to do.

I was using a sweet little .300 Winchester Mag that José had loaned me and while they all checked out the ibex, I prepared a spot among the rocks where I could get a good rest, just in case one of the ibex turned out to be a shooter. Sure enough, the head guide got excited about one of the billies that stuck his head out from behind some thick shrubs. I only caught a glimpse of him, but by the excitement being generated, I figured this may be a good one.

The ibex closed to under 400 yards, still with no clue we were waiting for them, when suddenly a different one emerged from the forest, closer to us than the rest, and José said, "That's the one you want, the one walking toward us on the right. Get ready and if he turns, shoot him."

Having absolute trust in what your guide tells you and knowing that when he says "shoot" it will be at a really good one is a rare event, but José Mallo is the kind of guy you can depend on in this regard, so when the ibex turned and gave me a better angle, I squeezed the trigger, without even analyzing the horns.

The impact of the bullet striking the goat made him jump 2 feet in the air before disappearing over the ridge with the rest of the troop. Not everyone, however, was as happy as I was with the shot.

"It may be a little too far back," José whispered as we began climbing to where the ibex had been, finding a small trail of blood, but not the frothy lung blood one would hope to find.

We followed what little sign we could, weaving in and out of the bush, hoping to find a dead ibex around the next turn, but not so. Cresting another hill, we spied the herd sneaking over the next ridge, but none of us could find the big one in the mix.

"He's somewhere down in that thick stuff, I'll bet," whispered José as he and the guides sat down to thoroughly scan the thickets where the ibex could be hiding out, or hopefully, dead.

I positioned myself so that I had a clear field of fire should the Beceite decide to make a run for it. However, if he did try and beat feet, it was going to be, statistically speaking, an iffy shot considering all the head-high brush and rocks he was going to be escaping through.

After an hour of not seeing anything, the guides all split up to get some different angles to glass. Soon, a low whistle came from José, who waved to me to come to him. For the first time in 2 hours, a glimmer of confidence shimmered in my soul as I crept over to where José lay glued to his binoculars.

"There, my friend, look to the left of the big pine tree. You see at its base, there is a tangle of branches? Watch those branches; two of them belong to your ibex."

After 5 minutes of staring hard at the spot José pointed out, two of the branches moved or rather two of the branches became ibex horns. A shot was impossible at the angle we were at. There would be no way to sneak a bullet into the jumbled mess where the wounded beast had laid up. The other guides as well as the mayor of the town, who had just joined our party upon hearing we had shot one of his trophies, gathered with us and began to "hablo" about what to do next.

Pushing him and trying to get him out in the open was soon ruled out due to the slim odds of hitting him as he ran through the terrain. Shooting from where we were was super-risky considering all the junk between me and said target, so when I suggested that José and I do the "sneaky-sneak" and leave the others behind to keep an eye on him and see if we could find an opening, all agreed to give it a go.

We had the wind in our favor, we had lots of cover, and we just needed to be as quiet as possible as we closed the distance from 180 yards to 110 yards. Getting that much closer still gave me no clear shot. A flanking move to the right for a better angle got us to 100 yards, but now the big pine tree was in the way, which became a good thing as the ibex couldn't see us as we crawled even closer.

At 60 yards, José looked over at me with a devilish smirk on his face and pointed to the right where a waist-high boulder presented a beautiful rest along with a possible perfect angle, although it would be an extreme downhill shot.

He waited where he was, while I crawled on my elbows and knees to the rock, eased the rifle over the lip of it, found the tree in the scope, and shazam, there was the ibex, his head up but nodding up and down as if the weight of his horns was too much for him to handle. He was in rough shape, but certainly not dead until I sent another round through his front shoulder, angling back through his heart and lungs, rolling him over at the impact.

I soon realized why the mayor had shown up, and soon a number of other men from town. They all apparently knew this monster ibex that I was now walking up to, his horns growing larger with each step closer, but lucky for me, no one had been able to find him during the limited hunting seasons in past years, one of those old critters that seem to disappear during hunting season. Everybody was thrilled, waiting their turn to finally get their picture taken with one of the biggest Beceite ibex ever taken.

If you could ever go from one extreme to the other, the next ibex tale would define that statement. Fall of 2010 found your humble

A really good Beceite ibex

scribe in Kirgizia with legendary outfitter Vladimir Treschova pursuing a variety of argali and the Mid-Asian ibex. Our local guide assigned to take us after the Tien Shan argali and ibex filled us in through Vladimir's translations that he really wanted to go after the ibex first, since he knew where a band of big ones hung out, with a couple of whoppers mixed in the herd.

He looked me over from head to toe as we sat around the table in his small but warm sheepherder's hut and pronounced to Vladimir, "This man should be able to get to the ibex. I had two Spaniards who gave up when they saw where we have to go, a man from Norway who would not cross the steep snowfield last year, and this year, two Frenchmen who shot small ones close to camp rather than going back to the mountain a second time. I tried to get the two other men last week to hunt them, but we had a problem."

Listening to Vladimir's recounting of what our guide said I asked if they were the two Norwegians we crossed paths with as we traveled into the area in a four-wheel drive truck, the ones who told us the tale of how two of their horses slipped in the snow as they crossed a dangerously steep hillside, tumbling head over hoofs to their death in the rocks below, breaking the horns of their hard-won sheep. Vladimir sipped at his tea and just nodded yes in reply.

Vladimir and our guide crossing a high mountain river

"No wonder they didn't want to go back up the hill."

A couple of days of fighting weather that made it virtually impossible to hunt, strong winds, cloud cover that shielded the mountains from view, and snowstorms with temperatures hovering below zero, finally gave way to clear skies and colder temperatures that would make an Eskimo shiver.

Mounting our trusty steeds in the dark, we left the camp in our wake under the flickering stars, five of us reaching the crest of an ice-choked ridgeline 2 hours later as the darkness turned a rosy hue in the eastern sky. Feeling the bite of the face-numbing cold, the head guide pointed to a sheer rocky pinnacle in the distance and yelled above the wind, "Ibex!"

I have to admit that I was somewhat disappointed in how much further we still had to go, as usually when you reach the top of a mountain, it's time to start hunting, but not today.

Asian ibex terrain where we shot the ibex

I got off my horse to walk for a while and get my aching knees stretched out while at the same time hoping I would warm up enough to find out if I still had toes inside my boots, since I hadn't had any feeling in them for over an hour. It didn't take long trudging along in the knee-deep snow to realize that the horse was a better option than continuously slipping and falling the way I was on the ice-covered shale. The horses seemed to have an uncanny knack of knowing where to place their hooves among the hidden shaky footing below the snow. I had the feeling this was not their first trip to Ibex Mountain.

After perhaps another 45 minutes of utilizing the spine of the ridge to guide us on our way, we stopped for a rest at a sheer drop-off that seemed to me to have no way around it and most certainly not on horseback.

The guides all dismounted, pulling out some of the ever-present cheese, salami, and dry bread for a midmorning snack, which I, by this time, could care less about, but my spirits did perk up when Vladimir pulled a large shiny thermos out of his saddle bag and poured us each a cup of sweet, strong tea that warmed the cockles of my heart.

A couple of the guides were glassing the now-closer rocky pinnacle that was to be our ultimate destination until one of them made motions for me to give them my spotting scope. After sighting in on what they were interested in, they let me have an anxious peek. The biggest band of all-male ibex I have ever seen were feeding three-quarters of the way up the pinnacle, casually browsing at the shrubs, moving en masse toward the top.

The youngest of the guides drew some signs in the snow indicating which one was the big one among five that were off to one side so I moved the scope and zoomed in on them half a mile away. All five were shooters, but one was much heavier and wider in horn with a dark shaggy coat, a goat you would surely remember the rest of your life!

When I made sign language to them wondering how we were going to get closer, they swept their arms out and around, saying that we would have to descend, then work our way back up to the pinnacle. I assumed we were going to walk until they all loaded up and began riding down the steep slope over terrain that no human, on horseback or otherwise, belonged on.

The Kyrgizians whipped their steeds mercilessly, forcing them through chest-deep snow across the side of a sheer hillside that was our only route to the pinnacle. The head guide's horse, plowing a path for the rest of us, stumbled and threw him over its neck at an especially dicey juncture, which made me take the hint and get off my nag before the same thing happened to me. At least I could struggle my way along the plowed snow canal that the first two horses had made, but this was still insane. Several times over the

A rare flat spot on top of the world

next half hour, my horse slipped, recovered, and then would lung forward, almost landing on the back of my legs.

Great, just what I need is a broken back up here in the middle of the Tien Shan Mountains.

I glanced down to my left when we spooked a flock of huge vulture-type birds and gray-headed crows that flew up from whatever they were feasting on several hundred yards below us. The guide behind me pointed at his horse, making a tumbling-down-the-mountain gesture, implying that the carcass was from the Norwegian's horse that rolled down the mountain last week. This updated news was all the inspiration I needed to really start paying attention to what I was doing, realizing what one wrong step could do to one's physical structure, especially if the horse took you with it! I held the reins a lot looser, letting the horse pick his steps carefully, figuring if Trigger decided to take a tumble, he was on his own. I made every effort to stay above him and out of harm's way as I led him through the deep snow.

I have to admit right here, and I promise you I do not write this without some consternation...I was scared, *really* scared. The worst thing was the Kirgiz men seemed to be just as afraid as I was, and they live in these frickin' mountains all the time! Step by fearful step, we plowed on through the snow. I sweated hard under all the cold-weather clothes I had on, but not wanting to stop and take anything off for fear of being left behind or falling out of rhythm with the others, I didn't.

The lead man came to a halt waiting for the rest of us to catch up as the junior guide gathered all the reins of the panting, sweaty nags. Untying my daypack from the saddle, my rifle still slung over my back where it had been securely beating the crap out of me for the last 6 hours, Vladimir and I followed the lead man around several cuts and chasms to a promontory where we were able to slip up to the edge, peering over at the full beauty of the pinnacle that rose in front of us.

Some of the ibex on the pinnacle had already bedded down for the day to chew their cud, others still milled about, nibbling at a few last tidbits before doing the same.

As we all glassed the hillside, searching for the big ones, Vladimir announced, "I see him. Look under the big boulder that has the tree growing out from on top of it. He is in the shadow below, in the cave."

Sure as hell, the big one had usurped the other ibex with not as much seniority and taken the prime bedding real estate all to himself. I didn't get too excited figuring we still had some hiking to do until the head guide said something to Vladimir, who then translated to me. "He says you will have to shoot from here. We cannot get any closer."

I looked at the guide assuming he must be joking, but the smile on his face and the way he was making the gestures to *go ahead and shoot, Yankee,* caused me to look at the ibex again, only this time, ranging his distance with my Leica binos.

"It's 478 yards, Vladimir, across a canyon and slightly downhill. I can't make a shot like that."

Vladimir related what I said to the guide, who said, "OK, then we go home."

The short version of the next 5 minutes is that I was right. Unfortunately, I didn't make that shot, but I did scare the hell out of the 30 or more ibex that, at the shot, all erupted over the top of the pinnacle. I assumed gone for good...

The head guide, hardly even fazed by the miss, grabbed me by the arm, pulling me along to follow him straight toward the spot where the animals had been bedded. Vladimir and the rest of the crew waited behind to let us know if they saw something from their lofty perch.

After 20 minutes of rough-and-tumble hustling across the cliffs and not sure why we were even bothering to go after them since I was sure they were in China by now, I called a halt to catch my breath. The guide was still smiling and motioning that the ibex would be waiting for us over the ridge. He made gestures showing me that the big one was old and blind and would not go far, *"So hurry up, Yankee, let's go."*

Off we climbed once more, gaining the ridgeline 10 minutes later, sneaking silently from boulder to boulder until the wily Kirgiz froze in midstride, waving his hand behind his derriere for me to catch up with him, quickly.

Easing up next to him, I saw the big ibex, no question that it was the same huge one, standing 200 yards away, slightly downhill, staring down the mountain at something other than us.

I hurriedly laid my pack across the boulder in front of me, settled in for a good rest, and let fly a quartering-away shot that felt good, but the animal gave no indication of being hit and the guide, scowling at me madly, announced in broken English, "You miss."

Second-guessing my shot and wondering what the hell was wrong, I chased after my running guide until we came to another cliff face, falling away to our right. He searched everywhere, swearing I'm sure at me as he mumbled to himself at our misfortune.

As he looked left, I was scanning the other direction when the ibex appeared from behind another small ridge not more than 150 yards away, so without bothering to point it out to the guide, I shot, hitting the beast solid this time, the ibex jumping at the impact and careening down the crevice, leaping from one rock to another until he came to a halt under a snow-free overhang. That was the chance I had been waiting for as I instinctively found him in the crosshairs as he stumbled on weak legs, the shot dropping him in his tracks, his carcass coming to rest in a small flat spot, thankfully not falling head over heels to a bad location as most mountain animals have been known to do.

I think my guide was actually happier than I was, if that's possible, as we made our way across some very hairy terrain to get to our waiting prize of over 50 inches of Mid-Asian ibex, hunted the right way.

Monster ibex

Stuck in Quetta

I WAS OK WITH THE fact that the weather had been lousy in the typically hot and dusty Torghar Mountains of Western Pakistan, 40 kilometers east of the Afghanistan border. I had remembered my rain gear; however, I will reluctantly admit to having left my long underwear hanging in the laundry room back in Seattle and would have paid a high ransom for them on day 2 when the skies cleared and the temperature dropped below freezing.

I was OK with the long bumpy Jeep ride after the hunt, leaving the mountains and venturing toward town, weaving our way through small backward villages of goat and fat-tailed sheepherders, wearing the distinct turban-ish headgear of the Pashtun people, those same people that we in America see on the television news most nights fighting along the Afghan border, some of the tribesmen siding with the civilized world's enemy, the Taliban.

When we stopped for fuel along the way, I assumed that the people who gathered and stared at us were doing so more out of curiosity than out of hatred. After all I could just as well have been a Pollack or German or Frenchman for all they knew, right? All in all, the drive was uneventful until we got to beautiful downtown Quetta.

I was scheduled to fly out of Quetta International Airport (consisting of a single two-story filthy building maybe 100 feet long and 60 feet wide, which does, coincidentally, boast a runway long enough to handle B-52s and F-15s) to Islamabad, and then from there I would be catching the next flight to Chitral in the northwest part of this game-rich country.

After our two, four-wheel drive vehicles were inspected at the armored security barriers set up outside the parking lot and we answered a few questions from the heavily armed guards, my handler (also guide, interpreter, and videographer) Ejaz told us to stay in the truck while he went in to sort out the tickets and paperwork.

I sat waiting and watching the sky over the runway as U.S. forces fighter planes made sound-barrier-busting practice approaches at the long strip, kicking in the afterburners as they sped off into the cloudy sky at Mach whatever, after each pass. We couldn't tell what service had their insignia on the tail of the camouflaged jets, but I felt tremendous pride in knowing the awesome flying machines were built in the "good ol' U.S. of A."

At each corner of the terminal building and parking lot stood a gathering of black-clad military types, armed to the teeth, keeping an eye on the entire goings-on in the parking lot. Since we were the only nonlocals in the airport receiving area, we seemed to attract more than our fair share of attention.

It dawned on me as we sat there waiting that if my memory served me right, the Coalition Forces had a presence in this area and the U.S. and Allied Forces were working closely with the Pakistani government in their struggle against the local tribal warlords and supporters of Osama Bin Laden and his fleabag cronies. The military force at the airport gave me a fleeting sense of comfort knowing we were at least on the same team, relatively speaking, albeit a heavily armed team.

I was still OK when Ejaz came out of the terminal with a sour look on his face and announced, "The airline pilots for PIA (the national and *only* airline in Pakistan, other than a couple of small regional puddle jumpers) have gone on strike, so no planes are flying today, maybe tomorrow."

Being delayed or plain stuck in a place you don't want to be in is part of the international hunting game and you have to go with the flow and relax, *'cause there ain't a damn thing you can do about it!* I used to get upset and cranky when things did not stay on schedule, but after enough screwups and delays beyond my control around the world and perhaps as part of the process of getting older (I was going to say "maturing," but that hasn't happened yet), I have attempted to accept the cards I am dealt and make the best hand I can out of them.

Our two handlers from Shikar Safaris, Serkan and Sard, and the six other people in our entourage all began jabbering and questioning what we should do next. I asked about driving to our next destination instead of flying, but the first response was "It's 12 or more hours on very rough road," to which I replied, "It's better than sitting here 'cause we have no idea how long we could be stuck here." To that, the local headman, Paind, who goes by the nickname PK, replied, "No way; it is way too dangerous to drive."

"Why are the roads so dangerous? Too much snow in the passes right now?" asked Dennis Anderson, my hunting partner on this leg of the adventure.

"No, there are many bad people, kidnappers, bandits, and terrorists on the roads who will not let us through," replied PK.

Well, that kind of puts her all in perspective now, doesn't it? I thought searching for Plan B.

"I thought I saw in a brochure at the hotel in Islamabad that there was a nice hotel here in Quetta. Part of the chain we stayed in the other night," I threw out on the table.

"Yes, that's where we will go now, and then I will check on flights and seats for tomorrow," answered Ejaz.

We all piled back into our two vehicles, leaving the security checkpoint at the entrance to the air terminal behind us and began the winding, congested journey through the ancient town. Thoughts of a hot shower, the first one after a week of hiking in the mountains, danced through my mind as grandiose dreams of somehow securing some beer, the forbidden fruit in this alcohol-free country, had me giddy at the mere possibility.

Driving in any town in Pakistan is a true adventure, but out-back towns like Quetta are a treat all unto themselves. The mix of donkey carts, three-wheel motorcycle taxis, semitrucks painted so outrageously they would make a hippie in a 1965 flower power VW bus jealous, honk, and vie for position along with goats, sheep, cows, and pedestrians on the narrow, filthy streets. A major disaster seems destined to happen at any moment.

Part of Pakistani drivers-ed courses must be that you are taught from day 1 to use your horn at every possible chance as it is the only warning that livestock or Homo sapiens receive that they are about to be run over if they don't get the hell out of the way fast! The phrase "common courtesy" has not made it into the Urdu vocabulary yet.

A half hour of zigzagging along cramped, high-walled back streets, weaving in and out of trouble, found us in front of a high-walled compound with a huge blue and white steel gate, that when opened after a series of "secret code honks" we drove through, finding a walled courtyard of tranquility in an otherwise dangerous town.

A German shepherd the size of a small horse stood menacingly secure on his thick chain, giving us the evil eye, hoping he'd be let loose for a taste of some Yankee rump roast. Wondering out loud to the assembled crew piling out of the vehicles what we doing here instead of at the hotel, the headman answered, "We stay here tonight." Then without a word, the hired help began unpacking all our gear and trophies from the trucks.

Ejaz leaned in close and said quietly, "It is much safer here than at the hotel. There is not enough security at the hotel, and unfortunately, there are some problems in the city right now. It is best if we stay here. It is much safer."

Glancing around the concertina wired compound, with its machine gun-toting guards and dog, a roof over our heads and knowing my needs are simple, safety always a top priority, I asked the million-dollar question, "Do we have a shower and beer here?"

"Yes, of course; anything you need."

I was OK.

I was OK with the rooms we were given in the large house and that the electricity was not working, nor was the gas heat on in the house. Third world countries are not renowned for having dependable infrastructures at all times, so I got settled in, sorted out my clothes, and found a clean set of pants and shirt, craving my first shower in a week, holding off on the beer as long as I could, figuring there was not an endless supply.

I was OK when I was told that there was no hot water for a shower since the natural gas was not working. I could get a good wash even with some cold water if necessary. I had a mental debate on just how badly I wanted a cold shower, finally electing to wait and hope that the natural gas would start working sometime soon. The cook was going to try to roust up some booze somewhere and would be back later. I was still OK.

What I was *not* OK with was some of the info we gleaned during dinner later that evening, at which time we were joined by the owner of the house, a gentleman if there ever was one and a very influential man in the region, with whom we discussed the success of the program he had begun in saving the Suleiman Markhor.

The conversation eventually got around to politics and the war in the region and when asked about why the power and natural gas were not working, he casually replied, "It is the work of one of the neighboring tribes. They are not happy with the situation here and have taken to bombing the gas lines running into Quetta and bombing some of the power stations. The railroad tracks were blown up yesterday. Rather nasty work and a real inconvenience, if you know what I mean."

No one said anything at the table for a few minutes. What could you say to that?

As I listened to the holy man chanting out the evening prayers over a cheap loudspeaker at the nearby mosque only a few blocks away, I said a fairly lengthy prayer to myself as well...

That was day 1.

Then there was day 2. No flights, wait it out, read, write. The power came on for a few hours so we could charge our laptops and iPods. Dinner consisted of some local spicy barbeque chicken and lamb with rice. It was very good. Our man in Islamabad, Farhad, worked all the angles as each flight got cancelled and he had to change our resos, trying to get us seats on the next flight. We tried to rent a charter plane. No luck. They had all been scooped up by the government.

Then there was day 3. Check with our contact and new best friend at the airport who was being promised large amounts of cash if he could get us on the first flight out of Quetta, but nothing was flying still on the third morning. Sit and wait, drink tea, read and write, be patient, stay patient, don't think about the bombs and the war raging nearby.

We had power for several hours, but no gas for heat all day. The temperature inside the house hovered around 55 degrees, still better than a tent in the mountains. I had heated enough water on a fire in the backyard to have a pseudoshower by this point, so the stench had dissipated, at least on me.

My laptop computer decided it wouldn't take a charge anymore, probably due to the converter being fried with the sporadic voltage and surges as the power came and went at will. Praise the

Lord it was OK later when we had a new round of electricity in the house.

Night 3 found even the locals having a cocktail after dinner. Not much was said around the room that night, most of the stories had been told, the jokes laughed at, secrets of past hunts revealed. We were all just killing time, each one of us in his own way.

The morning of day 4 came with the announcement from Ejaz that his contact at the airport said the strike was over and there would be flights today! Halleluiah, thank you, baby Jesus and Allah Akbar too. Things were looking up. Ejaz had somehow found seats for that morning's flight direct to Karachi from Quetta for Dennis and his crew. They left the house and me behind, all of us wishing each other good luck on the next leg of our adventure before they took off for the airport. My flight would be later at four in the afternoon.

Dennis called two hours later and said he was boarding the plane. "Good luck, buddy," he said with a joy in his voice that I hoped wasn't tainted with sarcasm.

The rain was pouring nonstop on the muddy streets of Quetta, rivulets of chocolate-colored water clogging the ditches of a town that does not see much rain in a year's time. People tried to go about their daily lives with blankets and scarves wrapped about them, not a raincoat or umbrella to be seen, as mud splashed up on all the bicyclists, pedestrians receiving a filthy splash from a passing car if they walked too close to the overflowing gutters.

We couldn't see the airplane at the airport when we arrived, but we passed through all the security checks, had the rifle and ammo duly inspected, bribed the right guys, and were patted down by an aggressive soldier so intimately that it was similar to some bad sex I've had.

We made our way upstairs and found Farhod waiting for us in the departure lounge. He had flown down to help us, just in case there were any problems getting seats on the PIA jet that we could now see parked discreetly on the tarmac, smoke billowing skyward in the distance behind it from an explosion of some sort.

"Thanks again, Jesus," I whispered, glancing out the window as the plane's tires screeched when they touched the runway in Islamabad...

Camp Raider of Moyowosi

AN AFRICAN PROFESSIONAL HUNTER'S daily schedule of catering to his clients' needs, fixing Land Cruisers that only breakdown at the worst time, managing a large staff of cooks, cleaners, skinners, and trackers, leaves very little time for rest. So when Minga, the head skinner in our Moyowosi camp in Western Tanzania, interrupted PH Schalk Tait from a rare midday siesta, Schalk was none too pleased.

"Bloody hell, man, what is it?" Schalk hissed from inside his shaded tent at the jabbering Masai.

"I am sorry, Bwana, but there is a big chui at the skinning shed, and we can't scare him away."

"You sure it's not that civet that's been hanging around?" Schalk quizzed him.

"No, Bwana, chui for sure. We threw some sticks at him, and he still stays there growling and won't leave!"

"Damn it. Just a minute, I'll be right there," he said as he swung his legs off the bed and began to lace up his Courteney's.

The boys have probably been smoking ganja again, the experienced South African PH figured, striding out of his tent into the scorching midafternoon heat. He cut through the open air kitchen, past the smoldering bread oven, ducked under the clothesline supporting the freshly washed hunter's clothes, before walking out onto the clearing where the skinning crew all stood behind a massive tree trunk pointing at the shed made out of thick branches lashed closely together with stout strips of bark.

Seeing nothing in or around the shed or skinning table, *just as he suspected*, he glanced back at the skinners' bloodshot eyes before he strode toward the shed to look for the telltale tracks that would reveal exactly who had interrupted his nap.

The rushing sound of leaves scattering next to the shed caught him off guard as a low-slung fury of spots charged full tilt at him, snarling its raspy threat as the big tom leopard swiftly closed the distance between them. Having not brought a rifle from his tent with him and suddenly feeling somewhat inadequate, to put it mildly, Schalk did the only thing that seemed sensible at the moment of truth. He charged toward the enraged leopard, raising his arms over his head and screaming an assortment of Afrikaans epithets, sure to get his mouth washed out with soap by his Boer mother if she ever caught him uttering such terms.

Luckily for Mr. Tait, the leopard either spoke fluent Afrikaans and understood the intended jibes or was intimidated by Schalk's show of aggression enough to screech to a dusty halt 10 feet in front of the PH. The pissed-off pussy lay growling within spitting distance, snarling for all he was worth as he crouched, lashing his tail menacingly back and forth before smartly having a change of heart and slinking back the way he had come, looking back over his shoulder and letting out an occasional screeching growl as he retreated. Reaching the backside of the skinning shed, the feisty chui gave one parting vicious growl before vanishing into the tall grass surrounding the camp.

The skinners all emerged from behind the tree laughing and pantomiming Schalk's show of force in the face of the charge. The PH joined the festivities with a nervous cackle of his own before

The skinning shed that the leopard charged from

turning and walking back toward his tent on shaky legs that he didn't want the staff to notice, praying that he wouldn't puke up his lunch in front of everyone.

I woke from my own comatose nap a half hour later, making my way to the dining area after standing under the cold shower with all my clothes on for 5 minutes in an effort to keep cool the rest of the blistering afternoon. Seeing Schalk sitting at the table sipping a Coke, a sly grin etched on his face, I had to ask the obvious, "Que paso, amigo?"

"There was a nice leopard at the skinning shed a half hour ago. I'm thinking perhaps we ought to throw up some bait on the other side of the creek and see if we can whack the cheeky bastard. What do you say, Mr. Smith?"

"Hell, yeah! Why not?"

We backed the Land Cruiser up to the skinning shed where we loaded into the back of it a couple of hindquarters from a waterbuck I had shot the day before. A stinking 5-gallon bucket of *matumba,* Swahili for guts and feces, was hefted in as well for added aromatic temptation at the bait site.

The trackers as well as the whole camp staff had heard the story of the leopard charging Schalk earlier, so the atmosphere in the back of the Cruiser was electric in anticipation of killing this camp raider.

Thomas drove the truck onto the main track leading out of camp before swinging it around the swampy area where the creek had flooded a small plain. Leaving the trail, the vehicle bounced along until Schalk tapped on the top of the metal roof, signaling Thomas to stop. There in front of us was the most perfect bait tree that ever grew out of the African earth. Sturdy trunk rising up to a thick branch sweeping off of it parallel to the ground, the tree was situated perfectly. No other trees for 50 yards in any direction, and a short grassy meadow below it.

No one said anything as they all went about their appointed duties; we'd done this plenty of times before. Schalk athletically shinnied up the tree, sliding out onto the overhanging limb. Barraca tossed a rope up to him attached to the buck's leg before Schalk yarded the meaty bait up into position, securing it firmly with a length of wire. Jumping down like a baboon on a mission, my trusty PH quietly said as we climbed back into the rear of the truck, "He wanted some meat from camp, so there's his meat. Come and get it, Herr Chui."

I chuckled at his remark and thought to myself as we drove off to search for our original goal for the afternoon, a bushbuck, that this hunt might have got personal all of a sudden...

After a couple of unsuccessful short stalks through some likely looking thickets where an East African bushbuck might lay up,

Thomas drove us back toward camp as the temperatures began to subside. Schalk leaned over the side of the truck as we neared camp and said, "Drive over by the bait and let's see if it's been hit yet."

"OK, but it's too soon. He will not be there yet," Thomas replied.

Schalk turned to me and said, "He might be right, but we may as well check since we still have quite a bit of daylight left, eh?"

I nodded in bemused agreement, happy to be along for the adventure as I glanced at my watch thinking it wouldn't be long till beer-thirty was upon us.

Coming around the swamp behind camp the truck lurched to a sudden stop 80 yards from the tree. Everyone could clearly see that the waterbuck had been fed on since we left it only a couple hours before.

Schalk quickly laid out a plan for everyone that Shabani, our other Masai tracker, would stay with us and help build a blind while Thomas and the rest of our entourage drove back to camp. He whispered to everyone to be as quiet as possible and hurry up.

We pulled out two pangas and two folding camp chairs from the back of the truck, then set about creating an impromptu blind, using a small dead tree as the first corner post. Shabani walked a hundred yards away to cut big bushels of long reed grass to fill in around the sticks and branches that my PH and I lashed into place with strips of bark and thick reeds. I swept out a clear space on the floor of the blind so we wouldn't be crunching leaves or sticks while we waited. We kept as quiet as possible, not breaking any branches or making too much loud noise, hoping Mr. Chui was sulking nearby waiting to reclaim his prize. Shabani showed up with one last load of thick reeds that we wove into the front of our three-sided framework leaving the back open.

"We have no time to finish this now. Let's just settle in and see what happens. If he doesn't come tonight, we'll finish the blind tomorrow. Get your rifle ready and see how the rest is on the top branch," he whispered in my ear.

I remember thinking as I made a channel in the reeds so that I had a perfect sight picture over the half-eaten carcass, *This is a far cry from the typical elaborate superstructures we build for leopards. I don't think there's enough cover under the tree for the cat to feel secure coming back to the meat. There's no way a leopard is going to return tonight.*

I swear to God I had just finished that thought when I looked away to see what Schalk was doing and noticed him looking at the bait through his binoculars, his arms tensed up as if something was wrong. I looked again through the scope to see what was up and there to my utter astonishment was a big male leopard standing above the bait, his claws buried in the overhanging branch, stretching his tawny muscles while he casually glanced from side to side for any sign of danger.

Our makeshift blind

A small branch poking up from the main one that held the cat covered his shoulder so I anchored the crosshairs an inch to the right of the branch, right on his heart, and squeezed off a risky shot without waiting for the go-ahead. The boom startled Shabani and Schalk. They weren't expecting me to shoot so quickly, I suppose, but I was sure the cat wasn't going to hang around long as exposed as we were in our makeshift blind.

Now for the fun part! Was he dead? Was he lying in a crumpled heap at the base of the tree, or did I miss him at 40 yards? Trust me, it happens to hunters all the time when the moment of truth arrives and your years of practice and skill building disintegrate into a blathering excuse-filled miss after seeing one of nature's most deadly creatures up close and personal.

Securing our headlamps into position since the darkness had suddenly descended on us, we waited a few minutes for things to calm down before we held our rifles at the ready and walked very slowly, shoulder to shoulder, toward the spot below the branch where a dead leopard should be waiting.

Not tonight though, *that would have been too easy*. We searched the short grassy plain around us for any sign that I had hit the cat to no avail until Shabani let out a low whistle 10 yards in front of us. We walked over to where he stood pointing at the ash-covered ground and saw a chunk of lung and a bloody spot the fleeing leopard had left behind.

I began to creep along the bloody path, my rifle at my shoulder, expecting a charge from the sassy chui at any moment, until Schalk grabbed my arm wagging his finger at me, like I was a naughty teenager or something,

"Let's wait for the truck. I hear them coming. They heard the shot in camp. I think he's dead somewhere in front of us, but let's not take any stupid chances."

I guess that's why good PHs stay in business, also known as "stay alive," because they know better than to let city slicker customer's testosterone control the decision-making process at critical junctures in one's life. Like when you are going in after a wounded leopard...

The truck showed up 5 minutes later, the new arrivals all excitedly jabbering away until Schalk told them all to shut up. Then we all climbed in the back, rifles and shotguns at attention, as the truck eased forward with the high beams on and Barraca sweeping the spotlight in front of us.

I mused to myself as we scanned the darkness with our petty beams of light that I was sure it had been a good shot. It felt right, it was a good shot, and I remembered the sight picture when I squeezed the trigger. Or did I jerk the trigger...?

"Ni pale, amekufa," Shabani yelled (It's there; he's dead) as his spotlight settled on the spotted back of the big cat 15 yards in front of us. We climbed off the back of the Cruiser, then fanned out to approach the fallen feline, just in case he wasn't "good and dead" like Shabani thought. But he was dead. The shot had been a perfect heart/lung shot. Even so, the enraged leopard had still run 50 yards, life pumping out of him with every leap, dead on his feet.

Pulling him by the tail, Schalk stretched chui out on the ground, then walked around to the business end of the cat, crouched down, and stared into the leopard's bloody muzzle, speaking to it as I stood watching with my .375 balanced on my shoulder.

"So what do you have to say for yourself now, you cocky bastard?"

Maybe it was personal after all.

Schalk and I with the camp raider

Brown Bear Surprise

For the people who have to live among them in Alaska, *Ursus Arctos Middendorffi,* the giant coastal brown bear (not to be confused with his smaller cousin of the interior regions, the grizzly bear) is a formidable foe who should be dealt with, very, very carefully. Sure, the brutes are bigger than a Volkswagen Bug and can weigh up to 2,000 pounds. Of course their open jaw can fully engulf a grown man's thigh, snapping it in half with canines that would make a lion jealous. The claws that protrude from the maw of a paw of a Kodiak giant can rip open an unlucky Sitka black-tailed deer from one end to the other in one lightning quick swipe. Sheer power exudes from these beasts as you watch them striding a sandy shoreline, scavenging their next meal, while making sure no rival dares invade his territory.

My not-so-limited experience with dangerous game around the world has taught me that if you spend enough time around their ilk, you learn in a hurry that an *unwounded* member of the "I can easily cash in your life insurance policy" gang are fairly predictable in their tolerance, or lack thereof, of you messing around the outskirts of their aura. Elephants, as an example, will let you get within 30 yards of them and tolerate your presence; lions, 80 yards or so; Cape buffalo, a more respectable 150 yards before becoming agitated. None of the ones capable of maiming, killing, or eating you are going to let you inside their comfort zone without someone paying a price for trespassing. All the bad boys are extremely predictable in this manner.

Not brown bears...

Take, as an example, the case of the California knucklehead who decided he was going to *live* among the Alaskan bears. He first tried it on Kodiak Island until the federal biologists ran him off, then he moved to the Alaskan Peninsula, setting up his tented camp at one of the beautiful parks that teem with the huge bruins as the schools of sockeye salmon make their final journey up the crystal clear streams every summer.

There he was, filming himself swimming with the almost "tame" bears, letting them walk up to him, close enough that he could touch their shaggy coats and even naming the various warm and fuzzy teddy bears he frolicked about with in the warm Alaskan sun-kissed days. That was until, of course, one of his "pets" smelled the fact that his menstruating girlfriend was in the tent with him and decided he didn't like it.

Eating the woman first (which was all caught on audiotape), the bear then moved on to our hero, the misguided Californian who didn't even have enough sense to run away, for dessert. I wonder what was going through his mind when his warm and fuzzy friends decided they didn't want to play nice with him anymore?

Anyone who has a cabin near the coast in Alaska for very long has had a brown bear do some damage to it. Everyone has a story. You will see bears on a regular basis around your remote getaway, fishing, scavenging, digging for roots or rodents, peacefully going about their daily routine, until one day you come home to your little love shack from the trials and tribulations inflicted upon you at your job in Anchorage and find that the man in the brown suit has crashed through your picture frame window, taken a bite out of every can of food in the place, ripped up the beds for no apparent reason, torn the front door off the hinges as he exited, but not before leaving a steaming pile of recycled salmon, berries, and beached whale on your living-room floor, guaranteed to make you vomit upon inspection.

I've been in on several of these toxic cleanups. They are no fun, but the curious thing is how much of the damage is apparently vindictive, nonsensical destruction they inflict. Almost as if once they get started, they figure they may as well get their money's worth and trash the whole damn place.

~

"Thank God the bears left the cabin alone this week," Justin Dubay, my guide for this brown bear hunt on the famed Alaska Peninsula, yelled over the racket of Rod Schuh's Super Cub taking

Our hunting cabin. Note the recent bear damage on the left side

off for Cold Bay. I could see where some recent repairs had been made to the one-room plywood shack that was going to be our home for the next 2 weeks. Walking around to the far side, I found a bear had made an attempt at getting in the day before, but must have changed his mind after gnawing through some plywood and 2 by 4s.

With a couple of Coleman stoves for cooking and heat, two beds with foam pads, and enough clothesline stung from one end to the other to dry out our soon-to-be soaked clothes, I was in heaven. Unlike lots of Far North hunts I've been involved in, where a two-man tent qualifies as shelter, freeze-dried food as your meal, and heat from a smoky fire (if you are permitted to make one, as sometimes the smoke scares away the game), this 12 by 14, 2 by 6 mansion was looking like the Ritz.

After unpacking, getting settled in, and putting the groceries away, we set up the spotting scope on the steps of the cabin to get a look-see at our surroundings, the perfect environment for bears if there ever was one, the Alaskan Peninsula. I gazed in wonder at a long, meandering stream with alder-choked banks that wound its way out of the snowcapped mountains before crashing into the North Pacific Ocean. The river held big runs of salmon in the summer and fall with hillsides filled with berries and shrubs, the bears' cherished diet for putting on fat to get them through their long winter hibernations.

"Tomorrow we'll walk over to that hill above the river and glass from there," Justin pointed out as he rose from the stairs to go into the cabin and start dinner. "You can see a lot of ground from that spot, and the wind usually cooperates. Now if the weather will just stay like this..."

The daily routine we soon settled into pretty much followed this pattern: up before dawn, eat some oatmeal and fruit, load up our packs, and hike to the aforementioned knoll and glass all morning. Have some lunch in a grassy nook, sheltered from the

The river on the left and the brown hill

never-ending wind, sneak in a midday nappy, then glass till dark settled in late in the evening.

We saw bears every day, however, no monsters of the dimensions the Alaska Peninsula is known for. We lost one hunting day due to weather so bad it made no sense to leave the warm, and more important, dry, confines of the cabin. We received a daily douche of showers and were thankful that we could hang our gear up each night, turning the cabin into a camo Laundromat.

After our day of lounging around the cabin, my tough young guide was restless and came up with the brilliant, if not backbreaking, idea that we should take a spike camp and climb the nearest mountain where he said, "We can see a whole new valley, and Mr. Big may be there. There's a couple of big bears living around here. I've seen them quite a few times. I don't know where they went, but let's go see if they moved to the next drainage north of here."

Justin Dubay-

The weather broke, letting us wade across the river and climb the mountain under sunny calm conditions. At a cut on the very peak of the mountain, I set up our two-man tent while Jason began reconnoitering the vast expanse in front of us.

Our view of the world from this vantage point was nothing short of incredible. Two valleys, miles of ocean beaches, a tidal lagoon, and a delta that had *brown bear* written all over it, gave us plenty to look over. So glass we did, and over the next couple of days we saw 12 male (or at least solo) bears. One really had Jason fired up, but he was moving fast, on some sort of a mission, leaving the valley where we spotted him before we could make any type of stalk on the big hairy bugger.

As much as I hated to leave our lofty perch, we were out of food, plus there was another angry Alaska Peninsula storm bearing down on us, the kind you didn't want to experience in a tent.

"We'll be lucky to make the cabin before that storm hits us," Justin said, looking over his shoulder at the black billowing clouds gathering on the not-too-distant horizon.

"Let's go then!" I replied, stuffing my pack with the tent as Jason crammed the rest of our camp into his.

Spike camp

Of course, we didn't beat the storm back...we got soaked to the proverbial bone when the rain and wind smashed into us as we waded across the river toward the warm sanctuary of the cabin.

The next morning we were up and at 'em at six, hiking back to our usual high point along the riverbank to glass the surrounding hills and bottoms. I liked this spot. I liked it a lot. It had a great deal of superb habitat to look over, and I figured it was only a matter of time until we saw one of the monster bears the peninsula is known for.

"Get your spotting scope out, Alain. Look at the bear just past the river mouth on that green hillside. Whoa, baby, this could be him," Justin whispered. I'm not sure why we were whispering since the bear was at least 2 miles away, but that's what guys do when they are hunting; they whisper. Justin found the bruin in the scope, then turned the power up to 60 for a better look.

"There're two of them traveling together. My guess is the blond one with the chocolate legs is a female and the dark brown one is the male following her, hoping for a little action."

I looked at my watch and realizing that it was Saturday, nodded in agreement.

Ah, yes, it's Saturday, and even bears must get lucky on Saturday night, I chuckled to myself, realizing that I wouldn't be getting lucky out here, unless my guide magically transformed into Heather Graham, who I am sure would look ravishing in a pair of green hip waders.

After looking at the pair through Mr. Swarovski's finest spotting scope, I had to agree with Justin that the dark one was enormous.

"Too bad they are so far away, eh?" I quipped.

"Oh, we can get to him. It might take us a few hours, but he can't go any further away because he's on the tip of a peninsula out there. Do you have everything you need?"

I looked to find the bears in the distance without the aid of binos and couldn't pick them out from the tundra. I wanted to say

Lookin' for bears

something like, "Did I tell you I have a titanium plate in my neck?" or "Did I ever show you my knee operation scars?" or the old standby, "Do you know how old I am?"

But I didn't. I just silently shouldered my pack, glanced back at the cozy cabin, sucked it up, and followed the young buck across the hinterlands. We followed the river's course to where it gently flowed into the sea, the plan being to wade across it at the mouth where it ran across a shallow sandbar. Good idea if the tide was not high...which it was, so we backtracked for an hour finding a shallow place back near where we started. Going this way was going to take longer than planned, but a guy has to do what a guy has to do, so we trekked on toward the tip of the peninsula.

Three hours later, after trudging across the wet, spongy mattress of vegetation referred to as "tundra" in these parts, we came to the low-rising hill we had last seen the bears on from our vantage point near camp. The wind was howling, the good news being it was doing so straight at us from where the bears were last located, giving us an added advantage as we looked for the bruin of my dreams.

As Justin led the way, slowly slipping along the side of the hill 50 yards up from the rocky beach to our right, I stayed right on his tail. Rain began to join the wind in its relentless punishment of our venture, so we stopped to don our raincoats and pants. As I was struggling with my coat in the wind, Justin crouched down quickly, and I obediently followed suit. I've done this show enough times to know that when the guide freezes in his tracks, ducks down, or starts to run, I immediately do the same.

"There he is! See him at the end of the alders? That big brown hump, that's him. I think he's sleeping. This is perfect!" Justin smiled as he looked at me for confirmation that I saw what he was talking about. Sure as hell, when I looked through my binos with the range finder, gauging him at 600 yards, the bear was having an evening snooze, resting up for his Saturday night action I figured.

"Where's the other one?" I wondered out loud.

"She has to be around here someplace. He won't leave her and will fight off any rivals if they try and approach her. Keep your eyes peeled."

I got my coat zipped up, tightened the drawstring around the hood, and looked cautiously around for the blonde with the chocolate legs. Nothing.

"Let's go. You ready? We need to get close and shoot him well, you understand? If he goes into those alders wounded, we'll have hell to pay, so we can't make any mistakes."

While I understood what Jason was talking about and respected his concerns, I also wanted to remind him that I've been around brown bears most of my adult life, including working on

Kodiak Island for many years. I've stood side by side with many a bruin on Alaskan rivers, watching them fish while I did the same, gladly giving up my catch that lay on the beach when they decided they wanted it more than me. I didn't have much fear of bears and felt they are way overrated in the aggression department.

Oh, and by the way, I've killed some lions and elephants and Cape buffalo, so relax, Justin, I wanted to say, but I kept my mouth shut and my ego in check, understanding that this man's job is to get me a bear and not get killed in the process, and he's a real pro, someone I had learned to really respect over the past week and a half.

As we started forward, some movement on the grassy hillside above us caught my eye. There, a hundred or so yards above and in front of us, was the blonde, ambling along, doing that pigeon-toed walk that big bears do when they are out on the prowl. I reached out and tugged Justin's coat to get his attention, pointing up to the big beast that had not yet noticed us.

"Crap! Let's hope she keeps going with the wind. If she gets downwind and smells us, she should run with the wind and stay out of our hair. Hold still and maybe she won't see us and screw up our stalk on the big boy," Justin said.

"That's no slouch-sized bear, either, is it?" I asked.

"Not bad. She's OK, but nothing compared to the other one."

I had to agree, but still the bear that continued wandering above us was impressive, especially the hide. Long blond hair on the back with a chocolate stripe running the length of the back and four dark brown legs tipped with claws the size of my fingers. Everything was going perfect. The brownie only needed to walk another 20 yards before catching our wind and then hauling ass back toward where we had hiked from, when suddenly, she raised her massive head, turning and looking straight at the two of us Nimrods, huddled in the short grass, wishing we had something to hide behind—besides each other.

"Don't move. She's not sure what we are."

It didn't take the bruin long to figure that whatever we were she didn't like us. The bear's demeanor changed from one of strolling around looking for something to eat to a huffing, stiff-legged shuffle that said, *"You are in my space, and I don't like it, and now I'm going to show you who the boss is."*

"Damn it. This bear going to charge. Get ready," Jason whispered as the bear got to a cozy 60 yards.

"Nah, she's just putting on a show. As soon as she sees what we are she'll take off," I jauntily whispered back.

"You got one in the chamber? You ready to go?"

"Yup," I replied double-checking my pet Winchester Pre-64 Model 70 chambered for the .375 H&H caliber. It felt warm and familiar, and if there was ever a time to have an old friend with you, it was now.

The bear stopped and rose up on her hind legs, swaying in the wind, trying to catch our scent, to decide if we were edible or not, I assumed. The bear was now parallel with us so our scent would not blow to the bear from the position she stood at.

The bear slumped back down on all fours, beginning to stomp its front legs on the tundra, a bawling noise coming from her substantial eating end.

She was getting madder by the second, realizing we were holding our ground and not going to run away from her scary display. She made a short rush of perhaps 10 feet toward us, then began the huffing and stomping routine all over again, working herself further into a frenzy.

"I've had enough of this," I said to Justin. "I'm going to scare her off, let her know what we are so she runs off. She's going to wake the other bear if she keeps this up. You ready?"

"What the—?" were the last words out of Justin's mouth before I stood up and waved my arms at the bear, holding the

Winchester in my right hand as I did so, a technique that has worked well in the past while fishing, causing bears to head for the hills when I act aggressively toward them. Yelling something about the bruin's mother's ancestry and cockily reminding her of whom she was messing with really got the bear's attention. The hoped-for result did not materialize as planned, my tactic failing miserably.

The now thoroughly enraged bruin was fed up with my shenanigans, tucked her ears back, the fur on her back standing on end as she began a charge from 30 yards away. Justin was already on one knee at this point and was screaming at me to shoot. I still actually thought the damn bear was only bluffing and would call off the charge at any second, but no, on she came, charging downhill as fast as a racehorse, her beady piglike eyes boring straight into my soul, an odd growl coming from between her popping teeth as she closed the gap in a split second.

Time to shoot, Mr. Smarty Pants, I realized as I slid the safety off and found the center of the bear's chest in the scope, pulling the trigger at the exact same moment Justin did. The impact of the two .375 bullets striking simultaneously staggered the beast, collapsing her front legs, tumbling the bear into a headfirst somersault before she miraculously came to her feet in one fluid motion, barely delaying the charge, and shaking off the bullets as if they were mosquitoes.

I didn't take my eye from the turned-down scope as I jacked another 270 grain Barnes into the rifle. As the bear regained her feet, all I could see was blond fur in the Zeiss—until an eye materialized, at which point my instinctive reactions took control and I shot again. The bullet caught the bear an inch below the right eye, smashing through skull bone, before entering the brain, halting the mighty predator dead in its tracks, a mere 8 yards from where my guide and I shakily held our ground.

Neither one of us said a word for a full minute until Justin looked toward the open hillside and broke the mood saying, "Well, there goes the big one."

I looked over and saw what he meant. The dark brown bear was running for a distant destination, never to be seen by us again.

We approached the blond bruin cautiously, making sure she was finished before I grabbed the rear leg to discover that the bear was a male. Not a monster, but at least a male. It now made more sense why the teenaged bear had come for us, since these types and sows with cubs are usually the aggressors of their race.

We took a few pictures in the torrential rainstorm that engulfed us before setting to the tough, greasy task of skinning the bear for a life-size mount. Reshuffling our packs when we finished to accommodate the bruin's heavy hide, I took on all of Justin's pack contents, then we loaded the bear's skin and skull into his, having to tie it all up with rope to get the 150-pound hide into one tight unit capable of being carried out on my guide's back. My load was less than half the weight of his and staggered me as I got to my feet to begin the planned 5-hour hike back to the cabin, which eventually took us 7 hours.

There are no tougher hiking conditions anywhere on the planet Earth than when you are trying to carry a staggering load across the soft, spongy tundra of Alaska. Every step is a nightmare as you cautiously throw one foot in front of the other, not knowing how deep you'll sink or whether the next step will be the ankle buster you dread. How my guide was able to pull off this superhuman feat was beyond me as I struggled with every step, resting often as the rain continued to drench us.

We stumbled into the welcoming dryness of the cabin somewhere around two in the morning, dropping our loads against the wall and beginning to strip off our wet clothes. Justin got the Coleman stove fired up for a little heat as I hung our gear up to dry on the

nails and clothesline strung about our the plywood palace. I pulled a stashed bottle of Crown Royal out of my duffle bag I kept under my bunk and without asking if he wanted one, poured the two of us each three fingers of Canada's finest into two tin cups. Handing one to the man who had been there to face life-threatening danger with me, I toasted him.

"Good job today, man; that was pretty wild."

"No shit," was his humble reply as we clicked trembling cups before draining them in one swig.

On the third cupful I added some instant lemonade to the cocktails since we didn't have any 7 Up to cut the potency as we sat silently in the small cabin, both lost in our own thoughts, reliving the charge and the questions of what might have happened. I noticed my hands were shaking still as I climbed into my sleeping bag, hoping the golden amber of Crown would help me sleep.

An hour later while still lying wide awake in the darkness of the cabin, a shiver continuously running through my body as I fought to think about something other than teeth and claws and fur, Justin's voice quietly said from the warmth of his own bunk, "Want another drink?"

"Yeah, I guess we better. I'm so cold I still have the shakes."

"Yeah, me too."

A Triple on Tur

OST BIG GAME HUNTERS I know would rate wild sheep and goats living on peaks and cliffs around the world the most challenging of all God's creatures. Yes, there is a thrill, an excitement; ah, hell, let's admit it, *gut-wrenching fear* involved in pursuing lion, buffalo, and elephants, along with several other species that bite back, but for my money, the physical and mental challenge involved in collecting the high-mountain species is the crème de la crème of hunting.

While admittedly, some of the sheep and goats, such as the Spanish ibex, may be quite gentlemanly to hunt and in some cases even enjoyable, what with the great food, lodging, and people involved, I'm talking about the species that live in the high-mountain regions where a good time is measured in the quality of the tent you live in for a couple of weeks and whether you run out of food...

Among many intrepid Nimrods, the pinnacle of mountain hunting is chasing the three closely related species of Tur scattered across the Caucus Mountains.

On the eastern edge of the mountain range where it creases Azerbaijan and Dagestan, you find *Capra cylindriconis pallas,* the Eastern or Dagestan Tur. As the mountains sweep westerly, one finds *Capra caucasica caucasica,* the Mid-Caucasian Tur, while at the extreme western edge of the range, *Capra caucasica dinniki,* the Kuban aka West Caucasian Tur thrives. The Caucasus Mountains'

247

Tur country

claim to fame, of being the steepest, nastiest, slipperiest, and dead-liest mountains in the world, has created the perfect sanctuary for the sheer cliff-loving Tur. It's such a tough place to hunt that not many hunters return for a second trip to the Caucus...

Our trip began when the legendary William Figge IV, known to his friends as Bill, and one of the huntingist white men on the face of the earth, decided one evening at the Safari Club convention in Reno, that we should hunt the two remaining Tur that neither of us had collected, in one trip! Oh, and while we are there, why don't we go for the Caucasian chamois as well?

The next day, not sure what I had agreed to the night before, we met up and finalized all the arrangements with the great Russian outfitter Dr. Vladimir Treschova, who assured us we had a "rea-sonable" chance of collecting the Mid-Caucasian and Western Tur, along with the chamois, if we could do a 3-week expedition into the Caucus Mountains.

"Most people like to do one or two of them, and then return the next year for the other, but if you want to try it, we can. The hunts are very physical, but you guys can do it. Sign here and give me a check," he said, smiling as we handed over enough dough to keep a third world country's economy in good shape for a couple of months.

Mid-September found us meeting up with Vladimir in Mos-cow before flying on to Nalchik, our hub for hunting the two differ-ent areas of the former Soviet Union where the Tur hide out.

First on the agenda would be the Mid variety, the crossover species that appears to be a blend of the Eastern Tur and the West-ern Tur. Their geographic location between the two distinctly dif-ferent species and the fact that the Mid shows similarities of both it's neighbors in horn confirmation and pelage markings makes this hard to argue with. But never let it be said that the record book committees would pass on making a category for a mutt species, so here we were to hunt one, "'cause you just got to have one."

The three of us left early the next morning from the lodge at Nalchik and drove 8 hours by 4x4 SUV until we arrived at a small cluster of stone farmhouses squeezed in on three sides by sheer mountain faces topped off with a velvety green patchwork. It took the local guides an hour to get the horses saddled and our gear loaded up before we began a 6-hour ride up the adjoining rocky canyon.

We set up a small tented camp under clear skies as the sun sank below the horizon, praying that the good weather would hold for a few days. The guides boiled water on a gas stove to make up a freeze-dried dinner, before getting to the mighty task of guzzling as much vodka as is humanly possible.

Bill and I, knowing the climb we had in front of us in the morning would be a ball buster, quit the vodka after one courtesy toast with the crew to the success of the hunt. The hooping and hollering of the drunken guides in the tent 10 yards away continued until just after midnight.

At 3:30 A.M. the sound of the teapot being dropped on the rocks woke us up. The plan was to be on top of the mountain at first light and try to catch the Tur while they were on the lower, gentler slopes feeding. I have to give the guides credit that even after partying all night they still all rallied in the darkness and after tea and biscuits we began the very difficult climb up the ridge behind camp on schedule.

The smell of vodka oozing out of the guides' pores was soon replaced by the stench of sweat as we worked our way closer to the main ridge hovering above us. We were in a good position huddled in the boulders, trying to stay warm while overlooking the canyons as the rosy hue of a new day brightened up the eastern horizon.

Bill's guide had taken him one way, while my guide and I went the other. I didn't see a thing in the morning, but Bill spotted a few Tur, although nothing big enough to be shot on day 1.

We all met at the crest of the ridge at midday, wolfing down some lunch, while the guides discussed a plan of attack. Two of the guides decided to go scout a far ridge while we were told to wait where we were. No sooner had they left us than here came a good male Tur, scampering down a rocky trail toward us. Since it was my turn to shoot and the unsuspecting goat was coming closer with every step, I started blazing away at the poor bugger as he scampered down the cliffs below us. Eventually the various holes in his hide had the desired effect of putting him out of his misery.

After the photo shoot, Bill, being an expert skinner among his many other talents, got to the task of getting the life-size skin off the great beast as I helped where possible.

It is a magical feeling walking back to camp with load of success on your back, arriving bone-tired and glad for it.

The next morning found us in the same position on the mountaintop, but the guides had a new plan to scout off to the right of where we had killed my Tur. We all worked our way along a sheer spine, cliffs of unknown depths falling away on each side of us. Since the guides spoke very little English, it was tough to figure out what was going on, but it became very apparent when the head guide suddenly ducked and hid among the boulders, excitedly pointing down the hill.

Bill positioned himself in anticipation of some action occurring at any moment when, sure as hell, a herd of some 50 male Tur came scampering up the cliffs toward us. Taking his time and looking for the biggest pair of the bunch, since we each had two licenses for these Tur, Bill whacked first one, then switched his sights to another big one, dropping them both stone-cold dead with his .300 Weatherby. We helped the guides with the vodka that night...

The next leg of our expedition took us east toward the Sochi region where we stayed in an old musty cabin that served its purpose

Mid variety of Tur

Guide packing out one of the Tur

well and certainly beat sleeping on the ground in a tent. Our quarry here was the chamois.

The first evening we arrived we drove to a grassy hilltop where our two non-English-speaking guides parked the Jeep and the youngest one motioned for us to follow him. Over the edge we went searching the cliffs and lush canyons below us for the petite chamois. Just as all visibility was about to vanish for the day, we

Bill holding on in typical Tur habitat...

spied a group of some dozen of them. However, knowing there was no way to get a clean shot at them at this time of day, we marked their whereabouts for our return at dawn.

In pitch-black darkness, we began our trek up the grassy cliffs toward where the Jeep had dropped us off. Storm clouds rolling in concealed the moon so that you couldn't see your next step in front of you. We climbed by braille.

Arriving at the place we had been dropped off at earlier, it was with some disgust that we saw the vehicle was gone. The guide got on the radio and spoke with his partner for a couple minutes, then began walking in a new direction. A half hour later, he got back on the radio and jabbered away in Russian before heading back the way we had just come from.

As the drizzle turned to rain, Mr. Figge and I were not too happy about wandering around lost in the dark. We tried to communicate with the young guide to tell his partner to turn on the car lights so we could see the vehicle, but we were not getting anywhere.

An hour of stumbling blindly about finally got us to where we could see the headlights. The taste of the first beer an hour later in the warmth of the cabin somewhat calmed my frazzled nerves.

The approach to the chamois the next morning was perfect until as Bill and I slipped slowly into position, our young guide sat up to glass the chamois, sky-lining himself and alerting the goat-herd which began milling around in the patch of green they had been feeding on. The jig was up, and we needed to shoot quickly before the chamois all disappeared over the mountain.

As I tried to find a big male in my scope Bill whispered, "Don't shoot. Your barrel is pointing at a rock!"

In my rush to find a target, I had inadvertently pointed the rifle at a steep angle into a granite pinnacle, and even though I could see clearly through the scope, the muzzle was blocked. God only knows what may have happened if I had pulled the trigger.

As I fumbled about trying to get into a better position Bill hissed, "I've got one. I can make a shot."

I was still trying to locate a good one and didn't want to screw up Bill's chances, so I quietly replied, "Take him!"

One nanosecond later, Bill's rifle barked, scattering the herd in all directions, except one big one that lay dead at the bottom of the canyon. I had no reasonable shot at the remaining scampering chamois.

I spent the next couple of days following the young guide around the slopes of the area but never saw another male, so Vladimir decided we should go to the Kuban Tur area where they also had some chamois, and if we didn't get one there, we could always come back after the goats had settled down.

The drive to the new area seemed to take forever, but eventually we met up with our new guides and the string of nags they had

Bill and his chamois

lined up for us. They haphazardly loaded the packhorses with all the gear and off we went on what they told us would be a 6-hour ride into the mountains. My sore butt confirmed that their estimate was correct as we rode into a small mountain cattle herders' camp at the headlands of a very beautiful canyon.

Unloading all the gear, Bill and I set up our own tents and put our duffels and packs inside, getting organized for next day's hunt. The guides, keeping up an apparent Russian tradition, proceeded to get completely hammered on the case of vodka that had been hauled in via nag.

Since dinner would be late, if it was made at all, Bill and I grabbed the hot water kettle off the dung-fueled stove and took it back to our tent and made ourselves a freeze-dried wonder that did the trick. I fell asleep to the banter of drunken buffoons stumbling about in the herders' shack 50 feet away from my tent.

Kuban camp

As dawn broke over the creek we were camped on, Bill and his guides started up toward the head of the canyon on horseback for Tur, while the aptly named "Spider-Man" and I left camp on foot to search for chamois in the cliffs surrounding the camp.

My 5-foot-2-inch tall hunting guide scampered up the shale and cliff faces like no one I have ever hunted with before. He seemed to have a definite destination in mind, because we never stopped to glass or search the area around us. We just kept climbing...straight up, with very few rests thrown in.

We arrived at a dominant ridgeline that afforded us a view in all directions 3 hours after we left camp and began searching every nook and cranny for our prey, which had bedded down for the day by the time we arrived in their bedroom.

Finding no animals where they were supposed to be, we moved a little higher on the spine until Spidey came to a screeching halt as his head snuck over a lip of the ridge. He crouched down and pointed over at the opposing cliff, excitedly making gestures that undoubtedly the new world record Caucasian chamois was waiting to be shot by "His Alainess," right now!

I ever so slowly slid my trusty .7 mm over the horizon, eyeball glued to the scope, but found nothing. I looked over to Spider-Man once again and shrugged my shoulders indicating I didn't see anything. He pointed over my shoulder at a tiny dark spot in a mattress-sized patch of yellow grass. I took another look through my 12-power scope and "sho' 'nough, der it was."

On closer examination through the Swarovski spotting scope, the minute head and shoulders of a male chamois gazing down over his domain became clear. His horns were hard to discern against the backdrop of rock and grass, but Spidey appeared to know this chamois and was very insistent we whack his ass.

I put the range finder from my Leica binos on him and found, to my dismay, that he was snoozing 462 yards away, with no way for us to get any closer either. I wrote in the dirt the distance for my arachnid guide, to which he shrugged, turning his palms up in the air, before making the "pull the trigger" sign with his nose-picking finger. While honored that my new friend thought I was capable of making such an impossible shot, I decided to wait and see if the tiny goat would get up and at least give me some more body mass to shoot at, or, God-willing, get up from his nap and jog a hundred or so yards closer and give me a fighting chance.

Two hours later the chamois had not moved...

Spidey nudged me as I lay under the overcast clouds, pointing at his watch indicating it was time to head down the mountain if we were going to get back to camp by dark. I began to stuff my pack, preparing to descend the cliffs back to camp when he tapped me on the shoulder and implied through universally recognizable sign language, "*Why not take a shot before we go?*"

To be honest, I had been calculating all the variables in my Swarovski scope with the built-in yardage-calculated crosshairs, wondering if I held the 500 yard line a smidge low, would it really work. I had a target the size of a teacup saucer at best to shoot at, but no wind.

I might as well try. I paid a lot of dough for Mr. Bansner's finest creation, and it's time to find out if it will perform as advertised, I thought.

The Bansner Grand Alaskan rifle has zero creep in the trigger, so I was pleasantly surprised at the kick when the 160 grains of Barnes Triple-Shock sailed toward its destination. To my guide's and my instant astonishment, the chamois began rolling down the hill, stopping 25 feet below its last resting place, 5 feet from disappearing into a chasm of immense depth from where it may not have been recoverable.

The trek to retrieve the chamois took us almost 30 minutes, arriving to find that it was dead all right and much smaller than Spidey had estimated. What else is new...?

We got the critter skinned out and all the meat loaded into our packs just as dusk blanketed the canyon. The slick, grassy cliffs took on new dimensions of terror as we made our way slowly back to camp, arriving at 8:30, to find Bill waiting with a super Western Tur strung over a corral fence pole.

Some tent celebrating was called for by the Americans in the crowd that night (luckily we had hidden a couple beers and bottles of vodka in our tent so the Russkies wouldn't drink it all), while the Russians, lacking in alcoholic inventory after the previous night's shindig, took it fairly easy compared to the night before.

The next day bright and early all the guides and I took the horses to the head of the canyon where, after reaching the summit, we began to glass for Tur. Bill stayed behind to finish off our skins, preparing them for the long journey back to the good old USA.

Seeing nothing at our first stop, it was decided that we would leave the nags with one of the guides and begin climbing to the top of the ridge to our right so we could check out the multitude of deep cuts and gullies jutting out like spokes on a wheel from the main ridge.

Up we went, busting our butts with each step. At times it was necessary to use your hands to grab a rock or tuft of grass to pull yourself further up. Two and a half hours of ass-kicking climbing finally found two of the guides and me at the top.

Rashid, the head guide and partying leader, pointed, implying through sign language where we were going, so I obediently followed, happier than hell that while high in altitude we were at least walking along the contoured ridgeline, working our way parallel to the canyon where our camp lay.

It was a long, frustrating day of seeing not a damn thing as we worked each canyon, searching the cliffs and crooks for one of the majestic beasts, but nada.

It wasn't until 4:30 in the afternoon, when the time was at hand to start our way down toward camp, that we finally saw our first Tur. With the naked eye, you could instantly tell it was a monster when he jumped from his bed and skipped down the sheer canyon walls, out of sight. Rashid didn't bother to wait for me as he ran like a two-legged goat across the shale slope we had just been clinging to, with yours truly running foolishly, full tilt, and right behind him. Adrenalin will make you do some whacky stuff, no?

As Rashid came to a quick stop, glassing the slopes ahead of us, I figured he was looking too far in front of us and that there was no way the Tur could have gone that far in such a short time. I searched the closer cutoff to our left and suddenly saw the big ram perched on a tiny ledge 200 yards away, staring at Rashid. I quickly found a rest on a nearby rock and shot at the ram, feeling good about the shot until Rashid yelled, "Miss, miss, shoot, shoot!"

The Tur hightailed it across the crevices and crannies, leaping from one rock to another until he finally slowed as he approached a skinny ledge he was going to have to dance across very carefully. When he hesitated, I shot again, feeling pangs of doubt as my guide once again announced at the top of his lungs, "You miss, you miss. Shoooooooot!"

At the yell, the ram leaped to the next ledge before bounding to a grassy patch of somewhat level terrain the size of a king-sized bed. Here he made the fatal mistake that many animals do, stopping and turning to look back before disappearing safely over the ridge, and when he did, I shot again as the opportunity presented itself. This shot crushed him. He staggered, fell forward on his chest, then rolled onto his side, never even flinching as I found him in the scope again at 275 yards, ready to give him the coup de grâce if necessary, but it wasn't.

The great ram was ours and on closer inspection, we found that all my shots had been good ones, the first two through the heart and lungs, but the pumped-up ram was still able to run until the last shot broke him down once and for all.

As we skinned out the beast, a herd of a dozen or more chamois appeared on the opposite hillside. Rashid implied that if I gave him some cash I could shoot another one, but I had mine already, and even though he was no monster, one was enough, and besides, I only had one tag. That didn't seem to bother the bandit Rashid as he took off after them to try and shoot one for himself.

The first rain of the trip at least held off until my guides and I stumbled back into camp around 9:00 P.M., wet with sweat, burdened with heavy loads, but about as happy as you can get.

We packed everything up the next day after Bill and I insisted we get going out of the mountains, especially as the rain was getting serious and conditions were deteriorating. The guides were all hung over bad after finishing off the last of the vodka, along with

My Western Tur where he came to his final resting place

some moonshine they had concocted, and wanted to hang out another day. By this point, we had enough of Rashid's B.S. and kept arguing with them until they agreed to head out.

On arrival at our departure point 7 hours later, Vladimir was there with everything organized, as usual, so we loaded up the vehicle and returned to Nalchik with its welcoming good food, hot shower, and soft beds.

As we celebrated our success that night, Vladimir proposed a toast, reminding us that we had accomplished the unheard of task of collecting two different Tur and a chamois each, in a total of 9 days!

"That, my friends," he announced to everyone at the diningroom table, "will be a record for the ages."

Taking Photos and Videos

I AM OFTEN ASKED HOW I get such great photographs on my hunts. "What's the trick? Any tips?" Well, I'm by no means a professional photographer, but here are a few things I've learned *the hard way* that might help you on your next adventure. For that matter, they will even be useful on your next family outing, where that special photo you take could mean a lifetime of memories for you and your loved ones.

Buy a compact, quality digital camera

Believe it or not, there are still people out there in 2011 using film cameras...seriously. I was on a hunt that cost the doctor I was with close to $20,000, and he was taking pictures with an old Kodak that was the same vintage my mum used for my birthday pictures in 1970. The copies of the event he sent me were absolute garbage, and thank God for him, I had taken still shots of all his animals with my camera so he had a decent record of the trip. There is no comparison in the quality between today's modern digital format and the old 35 mm film cameras for us rookies.

Buy the best digital you can afford, with the most pixels and the best lens. Even if you can't afford it, go ahead and buy the best one you can find. The memories 20 years from now will be worth every shekel you spend today.

I mention in bold a *compact* camera for many reasons. You will simply take more pictures if you have the camera handy at all times, in your shirt pocket, on your belt, or in a small case attached to a lanyard hanging around your neck, always at the ready. I learned from my African PHs long ago to hang my binos around my neck, with the strap under one arm, so that you can push them out of the way while crawling up on a likely target. I do the same with my camera case, hanging it under the opposite arm, out of the way, but available.

If the weather is cold, I simply keep the compact camera around my neck or in an inside pocket and it stays warm from my body heat. The most extreme example of this is 2 weeks on an Arctic ice pack hunting polar bears. Using this method, I was able to still get kill shots after a week or so on the ice with no external heat source. I just kept it under my clothes.

Another cold-weather tip: I also put the camera in my sleeping bag at night to keep it from freezing. That way, my batteries never die, *because they will if you leave your camera in your pack overnight.* If you are without any power source, your photo ops are done for the trip at this point...

I do have a beautiful high-quality digital SRL camera that I also carry in my daypack in Africa and places where I don't have to backpack with it. A trip to B.C. for sheep, where a large camera will most probably get destroyed by the horse, the rain, the cold, or the dirt, is not the destination for one of these.

I use the fancy one for posed or dead animal photos occasionally, say, in Africa, but truthfully, I can't tell any difference between this big camera and my small one, so it has spent most of its life in camp or in the closet at home. If you are a pro and it's a big thing to you, certainly take a professional grade camera and extra lenses along with you.

Carry extra batteries and flash cards

Keep the batteries safe and warm like your camera. If not, they will go dead just as fast as your camera. Digital flash cards are cheap and tiny, so take extras.

Pack a battery charger and electrical converter

If you have plans to hunt overseas, you must take a power converter suitable for your destination. I have one of the small sets that covers anywhere in the world, and although there are some plugs in the pack I have never used (yet), you never know when you might need the oddball one with flat wide pegs sticking out at unfathomable angles. Charge all of your batteries, including the one in your camera, before you leave home.

Take lots of photographs and videos

First, when it comes to taking pictures of you with your trophy, you simply cannot take too many photos. For every good photograph I end up with, I have taken at least 25 pictures. For every *great* photograph I've taken, there were probably 50 exposures.

Typically, there always seems to be something that's not right with a photo. The animal is not posed correctly, your eyes are closed, the shadow is wrong, you should have used flash, you are not looking directly at the camera, etc. Even the same pose taken four times will yield different qualities.

Don't let the guide or your hunting buddy rush you on the picture process. Take your time. Once the animal is down, the hunt is typically over anyhow, so who cares? Have them snap away from different angles, from down low (usually the best pictures are taken when the photographer is lying down), from up high, with all the trackers, some with the guide and you or your hunting buddy. Get some different poses, looking at the animal instead of the camera, the animal's head naturally posed on the ground, you looking off toward the horizon, etc. It's your hunt; you are paying an insane daily rate, so get as many shots of your hard-won trophy as you can. It's too late to redo them when you get back home...

Use a small tripod

Simon Camistral, the Swiss professional hunter, was the first guy I ever saw using a tripod for all his photographs, and they really turn out super. I now carry a small one that is only 8 inches long and has a Velcro strap around the legs that allows you to use the strap to secure the tripod to tree branches, your backpack, or whatever else is handy at the moment, or you can simply set up the tripod normally and snap away.

It's best to use the timer feature on your camera for extremely crisp shots. That way, your finger movement does not give the slight fuzziness that can occur on low-light shots.

There are many times when you do not have an experienced photographer handy, and rather than having someone cut your head off or not center the shots, you can set the camera on the tripod, center the shot in the lens, hit the timer button on the camera, run back to your preplanned pose, smile, and wait for the click of the camera. The tripod weighs only a few ounces and is a real benefit to improving the quality of your photos.

Keep your cameras in a Ziploc

Pack your camera, whenever it isn't hanging around your neck, in a gallon-sized Ziploc freezer bag to protect it from water and dust. Even if it's in your daypack, like in Africa where it spends the majority of its life, I still keep it in a baggie. The talcumlike dust of the Dark Continent will penetrate every nook and cranny of your digital and surely ruin it after 3 weeks of unprotected exposure to the elements.

Think about unique poses or scenes or random/nonposed shots

I constantly look through fellow hunters' pictures but find them all pretty much the same setup: dead animal with the proud killer squatting behind, holding the head up. So spice 'em up! Try some different poses, have some fun! Try some of these listed below. You may not like them all, but as Austin Powers would say, "Work with me, baby!"

1. Pose without your rifle in the scene.

2. Walk up on the animal, as if you just discovered it lying there,.

3. Stand behind the animal, with or without your rifle on your shoulder while you are looking at the camera. Stand but look down at the animal with respect.

4. Aim at the animal as if he's going to jump up and *git ur ass* at any moment, if you can get close enough.

5. Camp pictures showing the tent or lodge, bedroom, kitchen, outhouse, all add to the interest of viewers wanting to see what the trip was really all about. Photograph people sitting around the fire; get the fire in the foreground and the hunter sitting in his chair, drink in hand, being the bwana that he really is.

6. Photograph the staff, some of them working, in the truck, skinning, chopping wood.

7. Get airport pictures or even some on the plane. One time I convinced Mack Padgett to put on the British Airlines stewardess's little round hat in the first-class section of the plane while he had his BA-issued pajamas on. She was very accommodating (and apparently single by her reaction to the proposed pose).

8. Take live animal pictures. It takes many attempts to get a decent one, but they are fabulous when they turn out. Some of the digital cameras have good zoom lenses that really help, but you can always zoom in on the computer later and crop the photo as needed.

9. When taking video, rehearse or at least think about what you or your buddy are going to say in the next shot. Talking while being filmed adds a great deal of enjoyment for your audience, so if you can have a basic dialogue plan, you will see that your home movies are more palatable. You don't need any gory "Here we are gutting the moose" video either. No one wants to see it—no one.

A great piece of footage I always like to get is a walking tour of the camp you are staying in. Have your friend or guide film you as you show your tent, the cooking shed, the cabin, talk with the staff, ask them questions while filming them sometimes gives interesting footage. These shots give your friends back home a real sense of what it was like on your adventure.

Use forced flash

Especially on gray overcast days. Photos tend to be washed out at times, and colors don't stand out as brightly as they should. I now take every setup with and without forced flash. On the contrary, you sometimes have to turn your flash off when it's on auto flash so you can get the right lighting.

Take off your hat

The shadow created by the bill of your hat will ruin an otherwise great shot. If your hairdo is so bad that you have no choice but to leave your hat on, then tip it back off your forehead and use the forced flash mentioned earlier to brighten up your unshaven mug.

Face into the sun

Unless it is absolutely impossible, face the sun! Yes, it makes you squint a little, because *you will not leave your sunglasses on for a picture*, but it is the only way to get rid of nasty shadows.

Clean up the animal

Photographs of blood all over the animal's face or showing where the bullet exited look terrible, even to seasoned hunters. Remember that most of the people who are going to see your photos are not hunters, and the blood and gore disgusts them and will not endear them to our sport. It only takes a few minutes to clean up the critter and create beautiful memories.

First, move the animal around to the side showing the entry wound, which is usually the least damaged side of the trophy. If you have access to water, clean them up. Or use grass or moss to wipe away the worst of the muck, then use a few of the handy wipes and some extra toilet paper you carry in your pack for final cleanup.

If the blood keeps oozing out of a wound, stick a rock or two in it or a handful of dirt to stem the flow. Dirt comes in handy to thinly spread over really bad areas or where the blood has stained the hair and typically blends in with the animal's pelage since that's what he sleeps in every night.

If all else fails, you can always clean up your digital photos when you get home on your computer. The photo shop feature can fix a tremendous amount of issues, but it is still a lot easier to prep the animal correctly to start with than have to mess with it later.

Learn how to use basic photo shop on your computer

Cleaning up bloody spots on the animal, surrounding snow, or ground are just some of the ways photo shop can make a decent picture into an outstanding one. Cropping the photo to eliminate wasted space, zooming in on the subject and then cropping to size, deleting unwanted items such as a water bottle or rifle barrel, or even deleting your ex-girlfriend from your favorite Mexican fishing photo, are all easily accomplished on your computer. There are several different types of programs, and for us rookies, I think all of them work just fine with a little practice.

Review the pictures on the screen before you finish taking photos

After you've filled up some megahooty space on your digital dream collector, get the camera back in your stinky mitts and review the photos on the playback screen before the crew starts skinning your prize. Check out which poses look best and have more taken in that setup. Switch to some different poses, then review them as well. You might find that you need more background, or that the cameraman needs to get closer, or perhaps there are shadows from a nearby tree encroaching on your glamour shot.

Now you can change up the pose to fix whatever issue has come up. This is where having a large screen on the back of your camera comes in very handy.

All in all, your only true long lasting memories are going to come from the photographs you take in the field of your adventures, so why not make them the best that you can. Maybe your grandchildren will appreciate it.

Packing Lists

Sheep/Goat Mountain Hunting List

- Good quality "broken in" boots
- Three pairs of synthetic blend socks and liner socks
- Three pairs of synthetic long underwear pants and shirts
- Two pairs of synthetic fleece low-nap pants
- Belt
- Two synthetic lightweight shirts
- Two heavier synthetic zip-up shirts
- One light/medium synthetic zip-up jacket (depending on antici-pated temperatures)
- One compressible "Hollow fill" style liner coat for cold weather
- Quality lightweight rain gear pants and long coat
- One pair of lightweight leather/synthetic gloves and one pair of thicker cold-weather mittens, if necessary
- Fleece neck warmer (can be used as a stocking cap also)
- Sleeping bag and pad appropriate for temperatures you plan on enduring
- Baseball-type hat
- Binoculars
- Spotting scope and lightweight stand
- Range finder
- Bipod for rifle
- Passport, visas, health certificate

- U.S. Customs Declaration Form 4457 for rifles, if hunting internationally
- Digital camera with extra battery, charger, and extra flash card
- Daypack, waterproof
- Parachute cord, 50 feet
- Zip ties, 1 dozen, 1 foot long
- Name tags for trophy skins and horns. Can also be used as luggage tags
- Small, lightweight tape measure with inches and centimeters
- Small headlamp with a set of extra batteries
- Hunting belt long enough to go around your waist outside your coat to hold shells, range finder, knife
- Multitool with pliers
- Folding small sharp knife
- Small sharpening device
- Scalpel knife with extra blades
- Bandanas, two (mosquito repellent-imbedded ones are super)
- Shell holder, belt type or the type that fit on your rifle stock
- Rifle with sling
- Scope covers
- Ammo, 40 rounds in original box with protective wrap around it
- Satellite phone
- Electrical tape, ¼ roll for covering end of barrel
- Duct tape, ½ roll for everything
- Sanitary wipes (individually wrapped)
- Toilet paper, ½ roll, kept in a gallon-size Ziploc freezer baggie with sanitary wipes
- Small journal and two cheap pens
- Three large plastic garbage bags
- Mosquito repellent wipes (depending on climate)
- Iodine imbedded wipes, three. Use them on cuts, especially when skinning.

- Blister pads, a variety of Band-Aids
- Small Ziploc of pain pills, small soap, eyedrops
- Lens cleaners, individually wrapped ones are great
- Ear plugs, for sighting in rifle. Also for guides or hunting partner that snores
- Paperback book
- Camp shoes
- Electrical converters, if going overseas
- Extra large canvas/Cordura duffle bag for hauling capes and horns home on airlines

African Safari Packing List

- Binoculars
- Rifles
- Scope covers
- Boots with thick soles
- Gators, short leather or canvas ones, to keep seeds and thorns out of socks and boots
- Ammo
- Passport, visas, and health certificate
- U.S. Customs Declaration Form 4457 for rifles
- Camera, digital with extra flash cards and battery charger
- Electrical converters
- Shorts, two pair
- Long pants, three pair, consider zip-off legs
- Three long-sleeve shirts
- Socks, three pair
- Underwear (optional)
- Belt for pants
- Hunting coat (appropriate for evening temperatures)
- Camp shoes

- Toiletry items
- Rain gear, lightweight (regardless of whether or not it has rained there for five years, pack a set anyway. . .])
- Day backpack
- Hat, baseball type or a bigger one if you are sensitive to the sun
- Ziploc gallon-size freezer bags, six
- Hunting belt with ammo pouch, knife, and multitool
- Range finder
- Lightweight leather gloves
- Bandanas, three mosquito repellent-imbedded ones
- Sunglasses
- Clear lens safety glasses (for riding in the back of the hunting truck in the dark)
- Malaria prophylaxis
- Insect bite relief cream
- Journal and extra pens
- Small gun-cleaning kit
- Satellite phone
- Small medical kit
- Toilet paper and sanitary wipes
- Hand sanitizer, small bottle
- Lens cleaners
- Ear plugs
- Paperback books
- Duct tape, ½ roll
- Electrical tape, ½ roll
- Name tags with your info on one side and your taxidermist's info on the other. Include your broker's name as well. Enough zip ties to secure tags for all skulls and skins of trophies you may collect
- Headlamp, extra batteries
- Sun protection lotions

- Mosquito repellent
- Gun cases, soft ones

General Carry-on Packing List

- Passport
- Copies of your passport (put one in each checked bag also)
- Copies of itinerary (put one in each bag with passport copy)
- Extra set of travel clothes
- Prescription medicines
- Camera
- Binoculars
- One set of hunting clothes
- Hunting boots
- Quart-size baggie with deodorant, toothbrush, toothpaste, eye-drops, all in TSA-approved sizes
- Paperback books
- Satellite phone
- Journal and pen
- File with all documents
- Money
- Light sweatpants and T-shirt, or pajamas for changing into on long flights and for sleeping in on the plane. (Travel clothes stay fresher.)
- Sunglasses
- Medical evacuation membership card

While this may seem like a lot of weight in your carry-on, it is very necessary! I have had items stolen from my checked bag on several occasions. I have also arrived without my checked bag, but at least I had my boots, binos, and a set of hunting clothes and my sat phone in my carry on and was able to scrounge enough gear to continue the hunt. Could you imagine having to hunt in someone else's boots—*if* you could even find a size that fit you?

Basic Medical Supplies

- Band-Aids, small variety
- Anbesol, sore tooth and gum-numbing cream
- Eyedrops
- Cortisone 10 cream for rashes, bug bites
- Laxative pills - Can't start
- Lomotil - Can't stop
- Ciprofloxacin (a very important prescription for serious diarrhea and general intestinal problems)
- Iodine wipes
- Neosporin antibiotic cream
- Medical tape, small roll
- Blister pads
- Lip balm
- Sleeping pills
- Non-drowsy cold pills
- Nighttime cold pills
- Ibuprofen
- Aspirin
- Allergy pills
- Antihistamine pills
- Epinephrine injectable medicine (for serious allergic reactions)

Additional comments on these packing lists

Boots are the main tool you will use in mountain hunting. Buy good quality ones that fit your feet, are comfortable, are waterproof to a certain extent, and breathe somewhat. This is essential. I always buy ones with 400 to 600 grams of insulation because my feet tend to be cold unless I'm hunting in hot weather, which doesn't happen much in the mountains.

Buy boots with at least 8-inch uppers so your ankles are protected from sprains and rocks if you slide through shale. Good ones are expensive. The seams of cheap ones may rip open, the leather wear out, soles may come unglued, and the hunter's feet get soaked from rain.

Break your boots in before going hunting! If you don't, you will be sorry. There is no shortcut to this; it takes time, so plan ahead. I wear mine while getting in shape for a hunt, while I'm working in the yard, or when I go out dancing (just kidding).

Sometimes the outfitter will tell you to bring rubber boots or hip waders, especially if you are on a combo hunt, in, say, Alaska or British Columbia, but that's a different type of use than daily walking in the hills. Remember to break them in since rubber boots will quickly give you blisters.

For Africa or South American hunts, use un-insulated boots with thick, sturdy soles that can prevent thorns from penetrating them. I have seen hunts ruined when guys step on a thorn that penetrates the sole of their boot and breaks off in their foot, crippling them for days afterward.

Gators are a must in Africa where I use the low-sock saver type to keep seeds, thorns, and pebbles out of my boots. In many other wet or snowy areas, I highly recommend using the taller, knee-high Cordura type to keep the snow and wet out of your boots.

Clothing choices are up to you, and everyone has their opinions, but I have switched to all synthetics and use the "layered" approach for hunting in the mountains. The theory is that "if you wear layers of synthetics, sweat will wick away from your body," and it actually works.

When mountain hunting, you are constantly going from sweating like you are in a sauna, to freezing your hiney off while you are glassing, looking for Mr. Big. I find that I can easily peel a coat off, then a shirt, then a light shirt, many times ending up in only my synthetic underwear shirt while climbing. It's easy to pull them out of my daypack and put them back on, as needed, when I come to a stop and the cold sets back in.

Synthetics crush into a compact space; they dry easily in your tent or in the bottom of your sleeping bag overnight. Wool and cotton do not, *period; end of argument.*

Socks are similar. You need to be able to get your socks dry overnight, and synthetic, layered ones help stop blistering and keep your feet dryer than wool or cotton, especially with today's synthetic-lined boots that "breathe."

As far as **camo** is concerned, make sure it's going to blend in with the surroundings you will be hunting in. Ask around if you are not familiar with the area about what "pattern" will work best.

Stay away from too light of colors. Dark browns and greens are the best overall with a mix of black thrown in. Solid dark green and/ or brown outer clothing works fine in most cases. Avoid, at all costs, anything shiny or bright on your backpack or coat.

I prefer dull finish rifles and believe that the shine from your barrel or stock will scare animals away quicker than a foghorn.

A thin **camo face cover-up**, i.e., bandana or one made of see-through fabric, comes in handy on final stalks or when you are hiding in the rocks, glassing. Bill Figge, one of the world's great hunters, turned me on to using a face cover-up, and I've sworn by them since I first tried one on a Tur hunt with him. You can wear all the fancy camo that you want, but your face left uncovered is yelling, "Hey, I'm right over here trying to kill you!"

Regarding **sleeping bags** (get the best one you can afford), I have found that sleeping buck naked in them is the warmest way to go. I think there may even be a study out there somewhere that confirms this, or maybe I heard it from some pervert I was sharing a tent with, but I have found nude works best.

The other thing with disrobing completely at night is that if you put your synthetic shirts, pants, socks, etc., in the bottom of your sleeping bag by your feet, they will be bone-dry in the morning. Really...trust me on this. It works, and I think you get an extra day or two out of wearing them before your own inevitable stench forces you to either jump in a creek and wash the crude off or you give yourself a sanitary wipe "bath" after the first week, then change into something clean.

I have never burned a set of long underwear in the campfire after wearing them for a week, but have been tempted to on several occasions...

Rain gear should be taken on *every* trip, even on desert hunts. I once hunted the Gobi Desert of Mongolia where it had not rained for 9 months and a drought had been going on for 3 years. It was not the rainy time of year, so there was "zero chance of showers," the outfitter swore on a stack of Bibles to me. Regardless, I still took a set of rain gear, and sure as hell, halfway through the adventure, I got rained on for 2 solid hours on the top of a ridge 3 hours' walk from the horses. Unfortunately, that was where my rain gear was securely tied to the saddle.

Put your rain gear in the bottom of your daypack and always carry it with you. I prefer the light, rubberized *real rain gear* to the lightweight "breathable" style when it comes to mountain hunting.

If I am on top of a mountain or sitting skinning out a sheep or riding a horse for 7 hours in the rain, I want real rain gear that is totally waterproof.

I have seen the "breathable" stuff fail too many times, and the "quiet" stuff is pure garbage, in my opinion, after buying some very expensive stuff that failed miserably in B.C. on a 2-week rain- and snow-soaked sheep hunt.

Parachute cord comes in handy on every hunt I go on, whether it's securing a sheep to my pack, repairing a tent cord, hanging a clothesline up in the tent, fixing a broken strap on my pack; you name it, it's awesome.

Plastic Zip ties are great for miscellaneous repairs as well as securing name tags to the skin and skull of your trophy. I used to carry a small role of thin wire, which also works great but is heavier.

Optics. Buy the best you can afford and get the binoculars with the built-in range finder if you can, and then it's one less thing to pack.

A hunting belt is something I really like to use on all hunts. I hang my knife, a sheath containing my scalpel and blades (used for skinning; it's the best thing ever invented, and I rarely use my knife anymore except when boning), my multitool, and a 10-round leather shell holder on it. When I carried a range finder, I put it on there as well.

I secure the belt around the outside of my light coat so everything is always within easy reach. It's simple to take off if you are resting or napping, and all your essential tools and shells are always handy.

There's nothing worse than frantically searching through your pockets or pack for bullets after you've burned up the three in the magazine and the world record ram slowly walks away forever, over the ridgeline, while you are fiddle farting around.

I am a big fan of **gallon-size Ziploc baggies.** I put everything I don't want to get wet or dirty in them, like toilet paper, my journal, camera, socks, everything. *Especially when I am loading my daypack.*

If the pack happens to fall off the horse into the mud, if I fall in a creek, or the tent leaks and soaks all my *stuff,* I know my most precious things will stay dry, and in the case of dusty places like Africa, clean. Nothing will ruin your digital camera quicker than Serengeti dust.

Heavy-duty garbage bags can be used for a multitude of things, from putting meat in them before the meat goes in your daypack (ruining the pack forever), or putting dirty {stinkyer than a Taliban's turban} clothes in one before you put them in your suitcase for the trip home, or laying one out as a tablecloth on the side of the mountain to have lunch on it, or as a makeshift poncho. There are at least one thousand uses for them, and I never leave home without them.

Customs Declaration Form 4457 has become a quasi gun registration form, even though by law you do not need to have a license to bring your own personal weapon back into the USA. What the form is actually for is proof that you owned any valuable item before you left the USA and you are now bringing it back with you and are therefore not required to pay duty.

I remember in the old days you needed one to prove to customs that your Nikon camera or computer or expensive watch had been purchased in America, because at various times, it was cheaper to buy one overseas and then not pay duty when you brought it home. Now the form is pretty much only for firearms.

To obtain one, you need to take your weapon to the nearest U.S. Customs office and show it in person to an officer who will fill in the form with the weapons serial number, then stamp and sign the form. It looks very officious! You can put more than one gun on each form. Then make yourself **color copies** of the form to keep in case the original gets lost or stolen.

You will not get your rifle back into the USA without one of the 4457 forms nowadays, unless you find a very accommodating Customs agent, and they are rarer than the Dodo bird.

Many times in my travels I have had rookie airline agents at the ticket counter or even TSA agents ask me for my "Registration" or "Firearms License" (which are not required for any travel since there is no such thing for a rifle) and I have shown the imbecile the Form 4457, and it has sufficed to get me through every time. There is no sense in trying to talk to them logically or site law. Just give them your Customs Form 4457 and it works well, domestically and internationally.

You aren't going to get me into a discussion on **rifles** for the mountains or Africa, since the odds of winning anyone over to my opinions are about the same as Jacko being straight. Calibers, actions, barrel length are all up to you gun nuts to sort out. All I can tell you is the more I shoot a specific rifle, any rifle, the better I get with it.

The advantage to knowing your rifle and scope well is that when you don't have time to think, to gauge wind speed, distance, or find a suitable rest, which seems to happen a lot in the field, all that practice pays off when you drop your prey cleanly.

The only advice I will give is that lightweight rifles are fantastic if they can hold their accuracy after a couple of shots, which typically the very good ones do.

The other mountain advice I can give you regarding rifles is utilize a **bipod.** They take a little practice in getting used to setting them up quickly and they add some ounces to your rifle, but they improve your shooting skills so much that they are well worth the extra weight.

Innumerable shots of mine in the mountains have been in places where I did not have a rock to rest on. That is, my backpack was not high enough to give me the angle I needed, etc. I can name a dozen animals off the top of my head that I would not have collected when I did, had it not been for using a bipod.

Gun cases come in all sizes and shapes. Some have wheels, some are for two weapons, others are for only one, but in the end, all that matters is that the case is extremely strong. Do not buy a $50 case for your $1,000–$5,000 rifle! Buy one of the aluminum ones that will take a single padlock to secure it, or if you must, buy the ones that need two exterior padlocks.

Use combination locks that have the same combination code. If you use the cheap ones that have a built in key lock that comes with the cheap little key and you:

a. **Loose the key**
b. **The lock breaks from airline abuse**
c. **Something gets jammed in the hole your key goes in**

You are not taking that rifle anywhere until you find a new gun case because the various TSAs of the world are not going to make an exception for you, under any circumstance! Oh, and have fun finding a locking gun case in some crap hole country...

Pack light and take as little as you can into the mountains and in your luggage. You will be surprised by how little you can get by on comfortably.

Each time I go on a trip, I end up with items I didn't use and have not used for several trips, so I quit taking them. Items such as two knives, or four sets of clothes, or a case of beer (Crown Royal is lighter and takes up less space).

I will admit though that I do take Granola bars, some Jack Link Beef Jerky, and some candies along with me, since on most Asian and Russian hunts, the food sucks and an American snack will many times brighten up your spirits while breaking up the monotony of cheese, bread, and salami for three meals a day.

Hats. A brand-new safari-style fedora with a fake zebra or leopard skin band will cause lots of laughs behind your back (and some even to your face) from your PH and the local trackers when you arrive in camp. However, I must say that there is something extremely sexy about a good-looking woman wearing one. You might as well bring a pith helmet, while you are at it.

I usually take a couple extra green- or brown-colored ones to give to the trackers or guides. They like them, and sometimes it replaces the white one they are wearing which scares the hell out of every animal that sees them approaching.

I know you are going to develop your own packing list, and I encourage you to do so. However, let me reiterate, *take as little as you can on hunts.* You will be surprised by how much you don't need and how much easier it is to haul all your stuff around the world with you if you travel lightly.

Acknowledgments

I WOULD LIKE TO THANK all the hunting partners and friends that I have traveled with over the past few years who have made my hunting trips so much fun. I, unfortunately, do have to hunt alone quite a bit, due to conflicting schedules with hunting buddies and the fact that not everyone can go on a trip at a moment's notice. This tends to happen when new areas open or an opportunity arises that you *just have to go take advantage of*. It's never as much fun going alone as it is when are with a good pal, sharing a campfire and a cocktail under starry skies in some remote corner of this orb we call home.

I'd like to thank Dennis Anderson for introducing me to the hallowed halls of power at Safari Club International. Without him, I would still be sitting in the back row at the banquets, wondering who the guys are in the front row wearing tuxedos and the hot-looking women. The laughs Dennis and I have had on multiple trips together are memories etched in stone.

Bill Figge has taught me more about trivial animal and hunting factoids than I ever thought possible for a person to absorb in one lifetime. When I have a question about a species, its location, who's hunted one of them lately, who's the best guide to go with, why it is different than, say, another species, or any other minute detail on the animal I require, I simply call upon the walking encyclopedia of hunting: Bill Figge. Bill's hunting accomplishments are legendary

285

and his preparation before a hunt precise, making it always a learning experience traveling to oddball corners of the world with him.

Mack Padgett, of course, continues to thrill hunting camps with his sense of humor and dedication to making life as enjoyable as is humanly possible. Whenever I have to face something that bites back, it's always reassuring to know Mack is right there, safety off, taking care of business, no questions asked.

Shelley Mason, the most gorgeous creature God ever created, has accompanied me on several trips over the past couple years and has added a whole new dimension to the term "fun." Her positive attitude, her gift of giving love, her ability to roll with the ups and downs of travel, and all the while still remaining a beautiful lady, are incredible. Ever since our first date, the magic has never stopped.

Thanks to my two brilliant daughters, Nicole and Chanel, for all their support through the years and for still being there when I return from trip after trip. I hope the quality of our time together makes up for the lack of quantity. I'm sorry your dad is a vagabond...